TAMING THE SHREWD, ANOTHER HOLLYWOOD LOVE STORY

(ELAINE & ZACH)

Z.L. ARKADIE

Z.L. ARKADIE BOOKS

ISBN: 978-1-942857-34-1

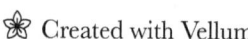 Created with Vellum

CHAPTER 1

ZACH LORD

*W*ith one eye narrowed, Zach Lord looked up at the gray sky. He was searching intently for something in the great beyond but had no idea what he was looking for. Or maybe he did.

Regardless, Zach felt way too antsy. It was ten thirty in the morning, a chilly sixty-two degrees, and sprinkling in LA. He inhaled the smoke from his cigarette, and the bitter taste made him scowl. It had been ninety-seven days since he'd sucked on one. He hadn't craved a cigarette until yesterday, after the call from Mike Falk, his uncle's attorney. A drop of rain dotted his open eye, so he closed it but continued glaring upward as he recalled their conversation.

He was in New York and had just finished closing another deal. ZYX Technologies had sold for double the asking price. There was a bidding war. One buyer wanted to gobble up the company and dissolve it to eliminate the competition. The other wanted to nurture what Zach's team had developed and make it thrive. Fortunately, after all the numbers were crunched—which included the three percent interest in the company that he would keep—the latter buyer had won the bid. So Zach was flying high as he strolled down Lexington Avenue while on the phone with Megan, his assistant.

He'd just told her to postpone his flight to Sydney since he needed to stay in New York for a few more days. An old acquaintance had given him a line on a new start-up that was seeking backing from his company. The guys who founded the business were young, smart, and pretty reckless. They needed someone with Zach's experience to come in and take their product to the next level. Zach couldn't wait to assess the situation. The bigger the challenge, the better their chances. Then his phone beeped. Out of sheer habit and without ever intending to answer the other caller, he looked at his screen to see who it was.

Zach stopped abruptly when he saw the name Mike Falk. That was his uncle Butch's lawyer. Mike called only when necessary, and what he usually needed was an on-the-spot expert opinion regarding the strength of a company they were about to invest in. Butch owned and operated BLB Wealth Management, one of the country's top investment firms.

"I'll call you back," he told Megan and then answered the other line. "Yeah, Mike."

"Hello, Zachary."

Mike sounded somber, which made Zach nervous. "So what can I do for you?" he cheerfully asked in an attempt to offset Mike's dreary tone.

"How are you doing, kiddo?"

Zach frowned. "I'm fine. What's up?" he asked.

"I guess it does us no good to beat around the bush."

"Beat around the bush about what?"

"Butch died this morning."

Zach stopped in his tracks and squeezed his eyes shut then opened them wide. Nope, he wasn't having a bad dream. "What?"

"Your uncle died this morning."

Zach felt choked by his collar, so he tugged it. "I don't understand."

"I hate being the bearer of this kind of news, especially when it involves Butch."

A face popped into Zach's mind. "Does my mom know?"

"No, I'm sure she doesn't."

Zach scrubbed his face with his free hand. His mom, Sarah, and Butch weren't particularly close, primarily because Butch didn't get along with her husband, Zach's father, Langston. Zach wanted to call his mother right away and break the news to her. She should hear it from him, but first he needed the details.

"How the hell did he die?"

"He'd been sick for a while."

Zach looked up and down the busy avenue, barely able to absorb his surroundings. "Is this a fucking joke?"

"I wouldn't joke about this with you, kiddo." Mike paused. "Your uncle had cancer."

"Cancer? No way. He would've said something to me or my mom if he had cancer."

"I don't know what to say to you other than you know Butch. He likes to do shit on his own terms. He was ornery in that way. But listen, we don't have time to rake him over the coals for being an asshole about this. Where are you right now?"

"Wait a fucking second," Zach barked. He needed a fucking moment. "Just wait."

Zach needed to sit. His head was spinning as he turned in circles, looking for a bench or patio table. There was nothing. Instead, he focused on the passing cars and the people whooshing by as if they had all the cares in the world, just not the same as his. Suddenly it sank in—his favorite uncle was actually dead. And of cancer? Butch was sixty-three years old. Sure, he'd lived on the edge. He ate whatever the hell he wanted and drank libations as though they were flowing from the fountain of life.

Women were his weakness, and his current wife, Betsy, was his fifth. Butch always married age-appropriate women, but he liked his side pieces forty years younger. But it wasn't the women or strong drink that kept Butch up all day and most of the night. Like Zach, his uncle was addicted to his work. The exhilaration of making a lot of money for his clients gave Butch the kind of hard-on no female in the world could ever inspire. So if any of his uncle's indulgences had sent him to an early grave, Zach would've felt better about saying goodbye to him forever. But holy fuck, he never thought he'd be mentioning "cancer" and "Butch Benjamin" in the same breath.

"Are you ready to continue? I don't have all day," Mike said.

Zach cleared his tight throat. "Okay, yeah." He wasn't ready, though.

"Listen, I don't want to be an insensitive asshole here, but you knew Butch. Business goes on even if he doesn't."

Zach stopped rubbing his eye. "I know. And I'm in New York today and flying to Sydney tomorrow."

"The funeral's tomorrow. I need you back here in LA so we can talk."

"Talk about what?"

"There are some details that need handling, and you're the only one who can do it."

Zach sighed sharply. "What details?" Changing his plans was the last thing he wanted to do.

"I can't tell you over the phone. I'll tell you tomorrow. The funeral starts at ten. The service will be held at the temple on…"

"Fuck," Zach said, rubbing his eyes again. "I don't do funerals. Butch knows that. He won't expect me to go." He stared at the passing cars as his eyes regained focus. It had just occurred to him that he was speaking as though his uncle were still alive, because no matter how hard he tried to come to grips with the reality of Butch's death, he couldn't.

"No problem. Then meet me at Mount Sinai cemetery for the burial."

"I don't do those, either."

"You're killing me, kid. Then don't come into the fucking service. It starts at eleven. I'll meet you at the gate of the mausoleum at fifteen after eleven. My secretary will text you the details. Be there," Mike said and hung up.

Zach made a beeline back to his hotel room. Once inside, he was sweating up a storm, so he stripped out of his jacket and damp shirt then downed a scotch on the rocks before calling his mother, Sarah. When he told her the news, she was quiet.

"Mom, you still there?" he asked.

"I am," she softly said. "I can't make it to the funeral, but I'll send Jean my condolences."

He jerked his head. What the fuck. "Jean was his third wife, Mom. He's now married to Betsy."

"Oh, well, I don't know her."

"Mom, are you okay?" She sounded indifferent about her brother's death, which wasn't like her at all.

"I'm late for one of my classes. I'll call you later." She ended their call.

That was yesterday, and she'd never called him back. He hadn't followed up with her, either. As he stood at the gates of Butch's final resting place, he was still wondering what in the hell was behind her reaction.

The rain was pouring down, but Zach wasn't compelled to seek shelter inside Butch's mausoleum, which was fit for a king. The building had to have been about fifteen hundred square feet. It was made of white stone and had columns, a domed roof, and golden double doors with stained-glass panels in the middle of each. He speculated that the inside looked like a scaled-down version of the Sistine Chapel, but there was no way he was going to verify his guess. He'd rather remember Butch alive and picking his brain for business tips while pretending to already know everything Zach told him.

Zach checked his watch then huffed impatiently. Mike was twelve minutes late. Zach walked to the nearest trash can to discard the rest of his cigarette. He decided to get back on the wagon while reaching into the pocket of his leather jacket for another. The contradictory nature of his urges hadn't escaped him.

"Shit," he muttered, scratching his forehead, then he sighed heavily and tossed the entire pack of cigarettes in the trash.

Butch's dead body was in that fucking mausoleum. He would never see his uncle again, and Zach thought that perhaps he should run into his uncle's final resting place and kiss his cold body goodbye. After taking a moment to check in with himself, he just couldn't do it. Dead bodies—and the spirits and shit that they left behind—gave him the willies. Now his uncle was joining the others in the universe of the unseen and unheard.

Zach had to get the hell off the grounds and was just about to race to his car, where he would text Mike and tell him they could meet later for a drink at Rocky's in Santa Monica or some other place of Mike's choosing, when a beautiful woman wearing a black business suit galloped past him. He had turned in time to catch a glimpse of her stunning face under the expanse of a wide black umbrella.

Zach couldn't take his eyes off her. The woman's skirt and jacket fit her sexy curves like a glove, and the scent of her perfume was sweetly alluring. Zach wasn't the kind of guy who lost his mind over beautiful women, yet he couldn't look away from her as she scampered past the iron gates and kept running until she entered Butch's final resting place. It took a few moments for the effect she had on him to wear off. He was about to turn away and text his uncle when he saw a man walking toward him from the back of the mausoleum. Zach couldn't see the man's face, but he had a familiar walk. The man raised a hand, and that was when Zach knew it was Mike.

The beautiful woman was no longer on Zach's mind as he walked toward Mike, but his anxiety was back as well as his extreme curiosity regarding what was so important that their meeting had to take place right then and there. The two men shook hands when they were face-to-face.

"How long have you been out here?" Mike asked.

"About twenty minutes."

"It's raining. You should've come in."

Zach folded his arms. "I don't mind the rain. So what's this about?"

"Cutting to the chase, just like your uncle."

Zach shrugged.

"Butch has made you trustee of his estate, which gives you…" Mike said.

He felt himself leaning away from the bearer of

news he didn't want to hear. "I know what it gives me." He suspected what Mike had to tell him had something to do with business, perhaps one last minor request. But hell, Butch had a wife and fucking Linus, his stepson, who was president of BLB. They got along. Why in the hell didn't Butch make him trustee? "Does Linus know about this?"

"Yes," Mike said with a firm nod.

From the look on Mike's face, Zach could tell his cousin wasn't happy about it. "What about Betsy?"

"What about her?"

"What did Butch leave her?"

"Nothing."

Zach snorted. "Fucking Butch. He'll eventually let the ladies know what they really meant to him."

Mike looked at him as though he couldn't give a damn about figuring out what Zach meant by that.

Zach shook his head. "At least that explains why she's not taking my calls." He had called her twice last night, before and after his flight, and once that morning. "But I don't have the time, manpower, or desire to run Butch's operation and mine too. But he knew that."

"I know. But Butch does what he wants."

"So what's Linus supposed to do?"

11

"You have to ask him. But Butch wasn't happy with his work." Mike put a hand on Zach's shoulder. "As you know, you can always designate another trustee, but…"

"All right," he said. "Then I designate Linus. Let's get going on that."

Mike was shaking his head. "He's not an option."

"He's an option if I make him one."

"That's not going to happen, and we can talk about a short list later."

"A short list?"

"Maybe Sarah…"

"No. I don't want my mother near Butch's business, and she wouldn't want to be near it, either."

"That's fine. But before we figure it out, there's one matter I need you to take care of immediately. It's regarding a talent agency, AMTA."

"What does Butch's business have to do with a talent agency? He stayed away from the entertainment and arts sector," Zach said.

"He had his hands in a lot of pots." Mike glanced slightly to the left then right, then he took two steps forward to get closer. "But I need you to disburse his shares back to the original shareholders," he whispered before handing Zach an envelope that had been tucked between his arm and the side of his chest.

Zach started ripping it open. "You mean sell the shares back to them?"

Mike put a hand on top of Zach's. "Not here. But we want you to get rid of them. No moneys should be exchanged."

Zach scratched the back of his neck. "Why the hell not?"

"It's what your uncle wanted." He turned and looked over his shoulder as funeral goers began pouring out of the mausoleum. "I have to get back. Come by the office in the morning to sign some papers. Seven o'clock."

Zach stopped himself from grabbing Mike by the shoulder to demand he be up-front about what the hell was truly going on between Butch and AMTA, but he didn't want anyone to know he'd been at the cemetery. Last night, he'd already held his own personal memorial service for his uncle. Before bed, he had two shots of whisky, one for Butch and another for himself. Then he sat for a long time, replaying good memories of his uncle as he tried to resolve all the lousy feelings that were stirring inside him.

It wasn't as if he were one of those men who

wouldn't let himself cry. He was just too angry at Butch for not letting anyone know he was sick. Plus, he wasn't ready to run into Betsy or Linus now that he'd heard why she wasn't answering or returning his calls. Butch had left her nothing, and she had put up with a lot of his shit over the six years they had been married. His uncle was a lot of things, but never had Zach suspected him of being that cold-blooded.

Zach would let Betsy grieve for a day and cool down a bit, then he'd arrange a meeting with her. He would give her exactly what she deserved, every-thing. So he rushed to his car and got the hell out of there before anyone could see him.

CURIOSITY WAS KILLING ZACH. HE TORE OPEN THE envelope as soon as he walked into his Malibu beach house. Last night, his flight had arrived late. He hadn't expected to be back in LA for a while, so there was no food in the refrigerator and no cook on staff. He had the Uber driver stop by Molto Famoso Subs so he could pick up a foot-long meat-ball sandwich for dinner. He'd eaten only half of it then, and since he was back home, he took the rest out of the refrigerator and warmed it in the microwave for a minute and a half. Now that he had breakfast and lunch on a plate, he carried his flimsy meal into the den.

He flopped down on the sofa and absorbed a view of the ocean. There was nothing spectacular about it, really. It wouldn't be worth much until sunset. That was when the view started living up to its multimillion-dollar price tag. Zach focused on the waves, which rolled smoothly into shore and back out to sea. Their movement was nothing like the rough couple of days he'd had. He took a few more bites of his sandwich then stared at the envelope. It was time to see what was behind Mike's bizarre instructions regarding AMTA shares.

Time ticked by. He was captivated by what he was reading. His uncle had purchased his shares of the company almost six months ago when the price had dropped to record lows. All the previous shareholders had owned stock in the company since 1951. There were six names on the list that Zach recognized, and they were men from families with old and strong money. Not only that, but they all had sold their shares to Butch within the same week.

"Holy shit," Zach muttered.

AMTA was losing nearly two million dollars a day without profiting. Zach immediately suspected an inside job since they were losing money so rapidly. Not even a public scandal could deplete a company that fast. However, he suspected Butch had known the company would recover at some point, which was why he'd bought the thirty-nine shares in the first place.

Zach knew his uncle well enough to recognize he wouldn't have bought straw unless he could spin it into gold. A woman named Elaine Hester owned the other sixty-one shares. Her profile, which was included in the packet, said she was a lawyer and a former managing partner at a prominent entertainment law firm in town. Even without any evidence, he knew she would like to own the other thirty-nine percent of the company as well.

He had no problem following through with his uncle's wishes by giving the shares back to the original owners, even if he knew the majority shareholder would get screwed in the process. He hadn't asked for the headache that taking over his uncle's estate would cause. He didn't want it. The sooner Butch's assets were out of his hands, the better.

To get the ball rolling, Zach had settled on calling his finance department and having them contact the original shareholders. Then his cell phone rang. Zach looked over at the screen. He didn't recognize the number, but it was local. Without considering who it might be, he tapped the green button.

The caller said her name was Elaine Hester and she needed to talk as soon as tomorrow morning. Since she actually had a hell of a lot to lose when it came to the business in which she was the majority shareholder, he agreed to meet with her.

CHAPTER 2

*E*laine Hester paced in front of the glass wall of her penthouse office, which displayed a view of the west side of LA. Every single part of her body felt jittery and tight, so she rounded her shoulders three times to get loose for her next meeting, one that was important as hell.

She had been walking back and forth. Elaine checked the time on her watch. Zach Lord was ten minutes late, and she was not the sort of person who tolerated tardiness, not even in a billionaire she'd never met or heard about until yesterday.

Although she had certainly raised an eyebrow at his last name. She wondered if Zach was related to Jack Lord, the man who'd just purchased her grandmother's multibillion-dollar real estate business only to absorb it into his own corporation. Were the Lords seeking to consume the Hesters? Had her grandmother pissed one of them off, and now they were on a quest to wipe them off the business map?

Elaine shook that ridiculous and paranoid thought out of her head. Imagining the worst-case scenario was something she did when the walls were caving in. It made her fight harder. She checked her watch again. Now Zachary Lord was eleven minutes late. She presumed that, like most men of his stature, he grasped the importance of being punctual. Her mind conjured up an image of a balding, ball-bellied man who wore a permanent frown from constantly pursing his tension-filled lips. That was the look of most billionaires she knew. She pictured him sitting in the back of his limousine, telling his driver to take his time, no rush, because he was sending her a message, which was that he was the one with the upper hand.

Unfortunately, she hadn't had time to conduct the appropriate research on him. Two days ago, Butch Benjamin, the man who owned thirty-nine shares of her company, had died suddenly. She still didn't know what had killed him. Perhaps his evil and self-serving heart had finally given up.

Anger and frustration raced through her, emotions she'd felt ever since learning more about what a sucker she was for purchasing AMTA a month ago. She studied her watch again. Butch's nephew, Zach, the trustee of his estate, was now twelve minutes late. She wanted to wring his neck. But then she heard her grandmother's voice telling her to use the extra time to do something constructive.

Elaine returned to her desk and looked over all her notes regarding her purchase of AMTA. The firm was the second-largest talent agency in the world, but with her at the helm, it could soar to number one. At least that was what she believed. It had been difficult to charge forward since taking over the company, but her next step would be the one that would get the wheels turning. However, she'd always believed an offer could be too good to be true, and that was definitely the case when it came to the purchase of her brand-new company.

Banker Dale Henley had given her a valuation, which presented sixty-one percent of the company stock as though it were a hundred percent. She didn't know that then, but he had found loopholes that legally allowed him to word the deal in such a way that he could hide the truth within the language. Normally, Elaine would've caught the manipulation and saved herself some grief, but she was given twenty-four hours in which to purchase before other buyers were approached. Granted, her emotions had taken over. Archie Rubenstein, the then-president, was running AMTA into the ground, and she knew she could manage it a lot better. Archie was the classic Hollywood scoundrel, with no business or creative instincts, but loved to use his power to get shit for free and sexually harass young women.

The day after Elaine signed the deal and wired the money to the bank, she learned not only that had she had bought a lemon but also that Butch Benjamin owned thirty-one shares of her company. Not too long after that, she learned AMTA was the victim of extortion by blackmailers who were running a sophisticated operation. Videos showed top-tier talent engaging in salacious, career-ending acts.

One casualty of the extortion was her soon-to-be brother-in-law, Jay West. Elaine would've been licking her wounds that very moment if Jay hadn't been valuable to mega media mogul Vincent Adams and his enterprise, AEE. The pre-release episodes of a new TV series starring Jay had been the highest-rated show a cable network had ever seen. No way was Vince going to allow scandal to ruin the acclaim and validation the series would bring his company. So he hired his wife, Maggie Adams, to fix the problem. Not only did she stop the extortionists, but she also made it appear as if the whole ordeal had never happened. Apparently Maggie was a secret agent of some sort.

Elaine was curious to learn more about the woman who'd saved her ass. But she had been too busy to connect with Mrs. Adams and invite her out for that drink Maggie had promised that the two of them would share one day.

Even though the criminals had been stopped, and in a deal to keep his mouth shut about the truth, Archie was now in jail on a lesser charge—rather than conspiracy to commit murder, extortion, and insider trading—it hadn't taken long for Elaine to figure out she had been set up and expected to fail. The extortionists were supposed to milk her dry, which would've forced her to sell her devalued stock to the first willing buyer, and that more than likely would've been BLB, Butch's investment firm. She never would've recouped the money she spent to purchase her portion of the company, nor her dignity.

It took another week before Butch would answer any of her calls. Then he'd agreed to come to her office on Wednesday morning. She was waiting for him and stewing because he was over an hour late.

At 10:10 a.m., she called his office and was informed that he had passed on Tuesday morning. Elaine could hardly believe what she was hearing. But she was in survival mode when she consulted the obituaries. She had already missed the funeral, so she hightailed it to the burial service with the purpose of figuring out who was Butch's beneficiary and arranging a meeting with him or her before the day was over.

Elaine arrived at the burial service just in time to see Betsy Benjamin sashay up to the casket during one of the prayers and spit three times on Butch's pine coffin. There was a collective gasp. Elaine's eyes widened. Not because of what Betsy had done—Elaine had heard Butch Benjamin was a womanizing cheater who had an appetite for barely legal girls—but because she felt Betsy's timing was off. She could've at least waited for the prayer to end, but then her actions wouldn't have been so rabble-rousing. Elaine had attended enough memorial services for men like Butch Benjamin to know that the widow didn't show out in that way unless her deceased husband had given her a reason to hate him. It rarely had to do with a mistress but always had to do with money. The gold leaf design, which covered all the walls, the white marble floors with gold swirling through them, and the solid-gold lampposts surrounding the pine box—a comical paradox at best—were evidence that a lot of that cash had gone to making sure Butch's ego was still alive and well, tainting the room even on the day he was laid to rest. Elaine's instincts told her that it wasn't Betsy's ass she needed to kiss in order to secure the thirty-nine shares she was owed.

After the service, Elaine had first tried talking to Mike Falk, who actually attempted to shame her for asking questions about business at the cemetery, in the presence of Butch's grieving friends and family. She could see his reverence for the dead was merely bullshit by the way his eyes smiled naughtily. He was hiding something, and more importantly, she suspected he was looking to blindside her somehow. So when she saw Betsy walk past Mike and look at him as though she wanted to push him in the grave with his client, Elaine knew there was an opportunity for her to figure out what the hell Mike was cooking up.

She was on her way to track down the latest Mrs. Benjamin when a guard approached her and asked to see her invitation.

"I'm here on behalf of the Hester family," she said.

The guard took a wide stance and crossed his arms over his chest. "This is a service for the Benjamin family."

She scoffed. "Are you trying to insinuate that the last name of everyone here is Benjamin?" She thumbed behind her. "Because I just spoke to a Falk, who I suspect told you to come tell me to leave."

"This is a private service for family and close friends only, ma'am."

Elaine narrowed her eyes and studied his intense frown. She could tell he was the kind of guy who didn't like being pushed around by women. But he also hadn't said another word, which let her know perhaps there was a way to make him see things her way.

"One moment." She opened her purse then her billfold and took out a hundred-dollar bill. "How about we make a deal?"

He scrunched one side of his face.

She took out another hundred-dollar bill. "How about this kind of deal?"

He grasped one end of the bills, but she wouldn't let go of hers.

"I'll give you this, and you get someone to stop the grieving widow from leaving." She pointed across the grass and at the black limousine where Betsy was at the back passenger-side door, speaking to a couple.

"I'll take that deal," the security guard said.

She paid him the money, and he ran off to stop Betsy's car. It all worked out. When Elaine told Betsy who she was and what she was seeking, the widow ordered the driver out of the car and told Elaine to get in the back seat with her.

Betsy's ice-blue eyes regarded her shrewdly. Elaine recognized that look. Heck, she'd trade-marked it. The expression was designed to convey not only that was she willing to wheel and deal but also that she meant to come out on top.

"You're very beautiful," Betsy said.

Elaine pursed her lips and nodded. Her response spoke for her, saying, *So fucking what? I'm here to play, win, and stay.*

Betsy grinned as though she was amused by

Elaine's nonverbal but very loud communication. "So, you want your shares?"

"Yes, that's why I'm here."

Betsy tilted her head to the left and studied Elaine some more. "You're very young, Elaine. How old are you?"

"Does it matter?"

"You look like one of those poor girls who came to Hollywood to become a star but failed miserably, so you became a lawyer."

"I don't come from anywhere but here."

"Yes…" She grinned some more. "I know you're Lorraine Hester's granddaughter." She shifted in her seat. "I didn't say you were one of those girls. I said you look like one. But anyhow, may I ask you something?"

Elaine was getting annoyed but knew she couldn't show it. Maintaining her cool composure, she nodded.

"Have you ever fucked my husband?"

Elaine kept her poker face. "No."

Betsy eyed her scrupulously. "That's right. You're a Hester. Your grandmother would probably disown you if she knew you were using your pussy to get ahead."

"My grandmother would never disown me,"

Elaine said brusquely, realizing Betsy had finally said something that momentarily broke her resolve.

Betsy paused and then chortled. "Of course, I see. Zachary Lord, Butch's nephew. He owns your shares."

If it weren't for the fact that she couldn't allow Betsy to see her relax, Elaine would've sighed with relief. At least she had a name. "Do you have his number?"

"My husband left it all to him. You see, Elaine, a woman doesn't marry a man like Butch for love or stay with him because she's devoted. Do you understand?"

The worst thing Elaine could do was answer that question. She had to convey they were not friends, and she wasn't empathetic to Betsy's gold-digging ways. "Zach Lord. What's his phone number?" Elaine asked firmly.

Betsy cracked a tiny smile, then she said the number so fast that if Elaine weren't so sharp, she would've forgotten it and had to ask again. She was sure that was what Betsy was hoping.

"Thank you," Elaine said and opened the door.

"Wait," Betsy said.

Elaine looked back.

"You want your company, then you get that

fucker to put it all in my hands, and I'll give you your thirty-nine shares. You'll pay nothing for them."

Elaine took a moment to study her and then smirked. "Oh, I'll be paying something for it."

"Zach is not Butch. Fucking him will be fun."

It didn't surprise Elaine that someone who appeared to be the typical kept wife had such motives. She'd met many wives like Betsy ever since she'd hit the big leagues in her career. What hardened them the most was learning they had kissed a frog and he was never going to turn into a prince or a king. No, the man she'd married was just a rich frog. And what the wife hated the most was that she couldn't delude herself into thinking she wanted anything more than his money, because every morning when she looked at him—at least on the days when he chose to sleep in their bed—she was reminded that she was in the relationship because of the standard of living he provided.

"Goodbye," Elaine said and opened the door.

Betsy grabbed her by the shoulder. "Or don't fuck him. You're a smart thirty-five-year-old woman. Convince him to give me what I fucking earned, and I'll give you your shares."

Elaine didn't say yes or no. This time when she

moved to get out of the car, Betsy didn't stop her. Perhaps she knew Elaine was going to think about her proposition and use it to her benefit if need be.

It was never Elaine's intention to interject herself into their family issues. She wanted to convince this Zach Lord to sell her the shares at a reasonable price, or else she would be forced to take him to court. But if that happened, she wouldn't be looking to keep the company—she'd be reversing the purchase. Her odds of winning such a suit were favorable. To emerge the victor, she would have to expose the blackmailing scheme. She wasn't ready to go that far, not yet at least.

Elaine stayed up all night devising a plan to get what she wanted from Zach. She wondered what Betsy meant by saying that having sex with Zach wasn't like banging Butch. Elaine guessed it sure wasn't like fucking George Clooney or someone of that stature. It was probably more like boning Jim Neely, the short little cocky, annoying agent who worked for her at AMTA. They used to be bitter enemies before she became his boss, and she had every reason to believe he was the reason everyone hated her so much. She'd finally fired his ass last week.

So she deeply pondered the question of whether

she could fuck someone like that to get what she wanted. Absolutely not. Seducing Zach Lord wasn't an option. She'd never used sex to get anywhere in life, and she wasn't going to start now.

No, she had to outthink him. She had to offer him a deal he couldn't refuse, even if she had to dupe Betsy, whom she didn't trust, anyway. There was no way the not-so-grieving widow was going to essentially give away an asset worth $1.2 billion.

At five o'clock that morning, two things happened: Elaine finally came up with a plan, and she fell asleep. Her alarm blared at seven. Elaine yawned. It was another day where two hours of sleep was all she was going to get, and that bummed her.

Finally, her desk phone chimed rapidly, twice, which let her know that it was one of her temporary assistants. Eden, her assistant of six years, was now in the agent trainee program, which put her in the mailroom all day long. Eden had reported to her regarding the effectiveness of the curriculum. As far as Elaine was concerned, the trainee program needed some serious revamping, and she would start the process of doing that very soon.

And Clara, Archie's former assistant—whom she'd kept on as her second assistant—was out yet again. This time she claimed to have the flu. In one month, Clara had racked up ten workday absences, which was alarmingly excessive. It was definitely time to replace her, but not with either of the two daft temporary assistants working Elaine's desk at the moment.

"Yes," she said.

"Mister… Um…"

Elaine could faintly hear Zachary Lord telling the assistant his name.

"A Mr. Zach Lord is here to see you." Even though he'd told her his name, the girl still sounded unsure about it.

Elaine closed her eyes as she shook her head. Why in the hell did she have the worst assistants in the building? She was the head honcho and should have had the best! "Send him in," she said tetchily and ended the communication.

Elaine stood then quickly sat right back down, preferring to sit. How she presented herself was important. She didn't want to seem too eager or weak. The objective was to strike a deal that favored her wants and needs, so sitting in the big chair made her look more dominant.

But when the door opened and in walked Zachary Lord, her eyes drank him in, causing her brain to turn foggy. He was a monument of a man, with dark, wavy, windblown hair that was conservatively styled. He looked as though he'd stepped out of a Giorgio Armani ad targeting high-powered businessmen. His chiseled jawline, sexy mouth, and brown eyes made her momentarily forget why he was standing in her office in the first place. And goodness gracious, he smelled good too. Elaine was actually familiar with the scent. She couldn't remember where and when she had experienced it, but it was recent, very recent.

"Good morning. Mrs. Hester?" His voice was velvety.

Elaine realized she had risen to her feet and reached out to shake his hand. It had not escaped her attention that he was asking whether she was a Miss or Mrs. "Good morning, Mr. Lord. And it's Ms. But why don't you call me Elaine?"

His lips pulled into a sexy smirk, and at that moment, Elaine knew he was the embodiment of danger. She had just come out of a bad relationship. The fact that she was attracted to him and was responding in such a way alarmed her. Only a fool couldn't see that after four engagements and breakups, her picker was off. So she took back her hand, because he was still holding it, and sat. Then

Elaine pointed that hand—the one that was so desperately missing their contact—at the chair on the opposite side of her desk.

"Please sit," she said, proud of herself for sounding as if she weren't having the internal responses he was inciting.

He was still smirking when he casually sat. "And call me Zach," he said, narrowing his eyes. "By the way, have I seen you before?"

"I don't know, have you?" She quickly wiped the slight but flirtatious smile off her lips.

Zach snapped his fingers and shot his index finger at her. "You were at the cemetery yesterday. You arrived late."

Elaine grimaced as she tried to remember ever laying eyes on Zachary Lord.

"You ran right past me."

Her frown intensified. "I did?"

"I was on the grass by a trash can." His voice trailed off as though he was ashamed of the admission.

She faintly remembered seeing a man. "No way. That was you?" He was smoking a cigarette. She never dated men who smoked. Elaine's smile returned because now she had a reason never to worry about being attracted to Zach Lord again.

"That was me." He winked at her.

She pursed her lips into a patronizing smile. "Well, I'm sorry for your loss."

He narrowed an eye. "Are you really?"

Elaine tilted her head as she tried to figure out whether he was joking. His curious, somewhat exaggerated expression made her err on the side of caution. "Yes, I am, certainly," she said, even though she had been ready to threaten Butch into submission in the meeting she'd scheduled with him yesterday. She had proof he was involved in the blackmailing scheme and deserved to be Archie Rubenstein's bunk buddy in prison, so he would have either sold her the rest of the shares for the price she'd paid for her sixty-one, or she would have taken Butch and his company down and gotten her money back in the end.

"Right," Zach said, looking at her as though he could read her thoughts. Then he shifted abruptly. "So…" He shrugged. "Why am I here?"

Elaine sat back in her seat with her fingers tightly folded in her lap. She struggled to maintain an air of confidence, knowing he knew good and well why he was there, but indeed, the ball was in her court.

"When I purchased this company, I was led to

believe that I owned a hundred percent of it, but—"

"You want my thirty-nine shares?"

She was caught off guard by his interruption. "*Your* shares?"

"They're owned by BLB, but as of now, I'm trustee of all my uncle's assets, and that includes AMTA shares."

Elaine opened her mouth to respond then closed it, fighting the urge to whine about how she had been duped. Then there was that smug look on his face. Zach Lord knew he was holding all the cards. The research she'd done on him revealed hardly anything beyond the usual. She didn't uncover any weak points. And how could that be? A man with his looks and bank account surely had a string of modelish girlfriends whose hearts he had broken. Those women always called the major gossip rags to snitch on their exes when the relationship went south. News of his uncle Butch's affairs littered the internet. But not so with Zach. Then Elaine remembered something she'd wanted to ask.

"Your last name is Lord. Are you related to Jack Lord of Lord and Lord Enterprises?"

"You mean Belmont Lord?"

"But everyone refers to him as Jack."

"I know what everyone refers to him as. Yes, we're related. Distantly," he said, frowning as though her question gave him indigestion.

She sat up straight. Now she was getting somewhere. "How distant?"

He paused, and his eyes narrowed slightly. "We're not here to discuss my family tree."

"Actually, we are. Especially since Jack Lord has bought my grandmother's business. And then Butch stole my shares. Are the Lords making an assault on the Hesters?" She didn't believe that, but she wanted to ruffle his feathers.

Zach tossed his head back and said, "Ah, I see." He looked her in the eyes. "Butch is my mother's brother. As far as Jack Lord goes, our grandfathers are brothers on my father's side. I've never met Jack Lord."

"You're both as successful as you are, and you've never met? I would say that's not smart."

He shrugged. "It's complicated, and I'm not here to talk about my family, if you don't mind."

Elaine certainly understood the complexities and pathologies of family. Her mother, Carrie Anne, came to mind. The last time Elaine saw her mother, she had just bailed Carrie Anne out of jail in Miami. Her mother had embezzled fifty thousand dollars from a used-car dealership she worked for. Elaine paid the owner of the dealership four times what her mother had stolen to make the charges go away. That was over two years ago, and she had no idea if Carrie Anne was dead or alive. She had spent most of her life worrying about her mother, but in recent months, Elaine had stopped giving a damn.

"I understand," she said. "Family's a sensitive subject."

He nodded gently. "I'm glad you understand."

She found herself staring into his eyes and turned away only when it occurred to her that he was doing the same.

Elaine looked down at her lap and cleared her throat. She wanted to fan herself, but that would've clued him in on the effect he was having on her. She needed to focus, get back on track, and get what she needed. She lifted her head, squared her shoulders, and showed him her take-no-prisoners expression. "So, I assume you came here with a price in mind."

Elaine was determined not to fold under the power of his intense stare.

"You are stunning. Do you know that?"

Elaine grunted, amused. "That sort of flattery gets you nowhere, Mr. Lord."

"I wasn't trying to flatter you, Ms. Hester. Just stating a fact." He sat all the way back in seat. "But now back to the shares. You want them?"

She opened her mouth to say yes. But did she truly want them? Did she even want what she had at the moment? Did she want the big, uncomfortable desk chair she was sitting in that once again was cutting off circulation in her legs and hurting her back? Did she want to walk through all the floors of the offices she owned, knowing nearly every person in the building hated her? It seemed as though all the plans she had for making the company more successful had been met with resistance. She hadn't gone a day without crying lately, and that had a lot to do with her ownership of AMTA.

Their gazes had melded. Oddly, she felt as though she had been sitting across from Zach Lord all her life. If she had allowed it, her eyes would've filled with tears, and she would've confessed all she was thinking.

Thank goodness her door opened and she had something else to focus on besides him.

"Zach, it *was* you I saw getting off the elevator," a brunette, the classically pretty kind with big brown eyes and a heart-shaped face, said as she boldly walked into Elaine's office and toward him.

Zach hopped to his feet and greeted the woman.

The temporary assistant was standing in the doorway with an expression of sheer terror on her face. "I couldn't stop her."

Elaine was too shocked to chew out her uninvited visitor or the temp. So she raised her palm at the assistant. "It's okay."

The girl quickly backed out of the office.

"Allison, what are you doing here?" Zach asked and hugged the woman loosely.

"Oh my God, Zach Lord, how long has it been?" Then Allison set her expression of wonderment on Elaine. "Sorry for barging in. It's just been so long since I've seen this guy."

She wasn't sorry. Elaine stood, intending to ask them both to take their reunion outside her office, but she was intrigued, slightly annoyed, and one percent envious—which was indeed too much.

"So are you in town? Or do you still live in LA?" Allison's eyes gleamed as she looked at him as though he were the seventh wonder of the world.

"I…" Zach glanced at Elaine. "I live in a few places."

Allison sneered. "Then you're still a hard man to pin down."

"You didn't answer my question. What are you doing here?" he asked.

"How about we grab drinks tonight and I'll tell you? My hotel at eight?" Now her eyes were smoldering.

Elaine couldn't believe the gall and shamelessness of the woman. She hoped Allison's desperate tactics weren't working.

"I don't know if I'll have time." Zach put a hand on Allison's shoulder. "But it was good seeing you." He removed his hand. "However, I'm in an important meeting at the moment."

"Oh," she said as though she had no idea she had just barged into the head honcho's office, and clearly for no other reason than she was hoping to get banged by the sexy specimen of a man standing before them. "I was just here on business, and I saw you, so…"

He frowned curiously. "You're here on business." He glanced quickly at Elaine. "What kind of business?"

Allison flopped a hand dismissively. "Nothing. It all amounted to nothing."

"You came a long way for nothing," he said.

"It's my job, but I planned on calling you later. Then poof, there you were in the lobby."

He folded his arms. "Call me regarding what?"

Elaine pressed a balled fist against her lips and cleared her throat.

Both Zach and Allison looked at her as if they'd just remembered she was there. Elaine didn't like how that felt but not because she wanted them to acknowledge her power and presence. Deep down, she wanted Zach's attention all for herself, and that wasn't good at all.

Allison rolled her eyes at Elaine and gazed at Zach with a flirtatious smile. "Have that drink with me so we can talk."

Elaine clapped her hands in front of her chest. "Excuse me, but you barged into my office in the middle of a meeting to make a date?" She faked a smile. "Leave. Now."

Allison twisted her mouth as she pointed at her. "Elaine Hester, right?"

"You know who I am. And you're blatantly disrespecting my position." She regretted saying that because she felt as though she was whining about not being properly acknowledged. Unfortunately, deep inside, that felt way too familiar.

Allison's eyes ran up and down Elaine's body, then she grunted indifferently.

Elaine struggled not to blow her top. She hated getting dragged into catty-land, and with her last comment, she already had one foot in.

"All right," Zach said. "Allison, leave."

"Drink?"

He sighed. "Yes. I'll call you."

She snubbed Elaine one last time before sashaying out of the office.

Elaine's blood was still boiling. "Really?"

He seemed confused.

"You made a date with her? And after she barged into my office?" She was pointing and flinging her hands wildly, so she enfolded her fingers tightly in front of her to make herself stop. After all, none of that behavior was going to help her secure the thirty-nine shares.

He cracked a mischievous smile. "You sound jealous."

"Well, I'm not." She made herself calmly take a seat.

Zach sat. "I'd be flattered if you were."

"I'm not, so… I'm fine. Let's continue." And she pasted on a smile just to show him.

After a moment, Zach also sat. "I see she's going to be a problem for us."

"About the shares…" And then what he'd said finally sank in. "Us?" Elaine asked.

"I'm keeping the shares."

She could hardly believe what she was hearing. "You?"

"Yeah, sure. Why not?" He crossed his legs in a confident manner that matched his cocky smile.

Elaine jerked her neck. "Why not? Because this is my life." She nudged herself in the chest. "I've sunk every dime I've had into this business, not to mention my blood sweat and tears, and you just willy-nilly decide you want to be a co-owner? No way."

He took a moment to study her then leaned toward her. "When someone like Allison is sniffing around your business, then you want someone like me in your corner, Elaine."

She shifted her body toward him until their faces were closer. "I can handle someone like Allison on my own."

He didn't back away. "I have no doubt you can, but you don't have to because I'm here, and I'm not going anywhere." He sat back and crossed his legs again.

Finally, she sighed and sat back as well. "Okay, then. What's your endgame?"

For a moment, it looked as though he was undressing her with his eyes. But then he finally put a fist over his mouth and cleared his throat. "I want you to trust me, and I want us to work as a team. But I also want you to realize how fucking valuable I am to you right now."

Elaine had to remember to breathe. The way he was looking at her, what he had just said... She wanted to strip her clothes off and let him bang her brains out. What the hell was wrong with her? She wasn't that type of girl. A man had to work to get in her pants. He had to make her feel special. Yes, she'd had four fiancés, but she'd rarely had sex with any of them, and she'd done it only twice with Gary, the fiancé who fucked her over. She wasn't big on sex. She didn't think the act had anything to do with having a satisfying relationship. Plus, she'd heard about orgasms, but no man had ever given her one.

Once, she had confessed this to her cousin Theresa, and two days later, a vibrator arrived at her house. Elaine had no idea why she never used the thing, but at the moment, she was wondering if

Zach was the man who would make her want to toss it in the garbage.

She opened her mouth to beg him to please walk out of her office and never come back. She was way too attracted to him and had sworn off men. Also, she had the worst picker in the world, which meant that beneath all of his magnificence, Zach was probably another dud. However, her business instincts had to clobber her romantic tendencies. A man with his sort of expertise could really help her get AMTA on the right track. Plus that gave her more time to learn his weaknesses so she could take full control of her company. So Elaine did exactly what would be expected of Lorraine Hester's granddaughter. She held out her hand.

"Deal," she said.

He shook her hand, and she became lightheaded.

After a moment of pause, he flexed his eyebrows at her. "Deal."

CHAPTER 3

ZACH LORD

*H*e was crazy, that was for sure. Zach adhered to a pretty tight schedule, and he had no room in it to add the duties that came with running a talent agency. But something about Elaine Hester inspired the same kind of hard-on he'd had after closing the sale of ZYX Technologies. Fairly early on in their meeting, he had decided to go against his uncle Butch's wishes and give her the thirty-nine shares in exchange for a date. He didn't need the shares or want them.

When Allison showed up, Zach suspected Elaine's company was headed for the sort of trouble she wouldn't see coming until it was too late, and that was when he knew he had to stay. Allison Johnson of Blue Star Capital would grace the halls of a company as volatile as AMTA only if she were there to steal it right out from under Elaine.

Zach walked behind Elaine as she escorted him to the HR department, where he was to be granted owner's access. He couldn't take his eyes off her figure, and her nearness excited him. To calm himself, he looked around the open floor, where all the cubicles were placed. All eyes were on them. Most were intrigued. He also noticed that a number of the offices they passed were empty.

"Not at full capacity?" he asked.

"What?" Elaine snapped.

"There are lots of empty offices."

She stopped in her tracks. "Are you sure you want to do this?"

He frowned curiously. "Do what?"

"Be here. Don't you have a corporation to run?"

Zach had wondered what in the hell he was doing. He should've been on a flight back to New York, where he would later meet with Founders Technology, and after that he'd be off to Sydney. His team could function without him, but it was his expertise that made his company so successful. He had no idea how to run a talent agency, especially one headquartered in Hollywood.

"Don't worry about me. I won't get in your way."

"Okay, then, why don't you call me once a week for an update or something. Or I can send reports to your office. How about that?"

The look in her eyes was so damn sexy. It was vulnerable yet strong and also mischievous. He wondered what expressions her face would hold when he finally tasted her mouth and skin.

She snapped her fingers. "Are you still with me?"

He shook his head. "I'm here, Elaine. I'm not going anywhere. I can find my way to HR, if you have something else you would like to do."

He bet she didn't know she was pouting. And it took everything inside him not to throw her against the wall and feverishly kiss her sexy lips.

She started walking again, and he followed her for about ten more feet before she stopped at the receptionist's desk and asked the woman behind it to show him to HR.

"Have a nice day, Zach. Let my assistant… me, let me know if you need anything else."

She walked away.

"Elaine?"

She stopped and looked back. Their eyes connected.

Her pretty face made him smile. "I will."

She grimaced. "You will what?"

"I'll let you know if I need something."

Her mouth opened then closed. Elaine nodded jerkily before continuing on her way.

As soon as she was out of sight, he released the tension in his body.

From that point on, Zach was given the star treatment. He had a key to the executive elevator and access to every part of the building that belonged to AMTA. A badge was made up for him on the spot. The company wanted to give him three assistants, but he already had his two assistants, Megan and Julie, so he asked AMTA to set up parking spaces and access badges for them. As far as the business of his own company, Mega Link Venture Group, the show must go on, and he needed his assistants nearby.

Lorna Kelsey, the director of HR, escorted him to an executive office she said he might be interested in. By the time they entered the elevator, he already knew he wasn't interested in that office because it was too far from Elaine's. However, he did want to continue the journey with her. It was an opportunity to learn whether Lorna knew why Allison had been there.

"So how is the general mood around here?" he asked.

"Not good." She didn't even turn to look at him when she spoke.

"And why is that?"

"We had a change of ownership, and the new owner has decided to come in and leave her mark."

Zach detected the sarcasm. "Are you referring to Elaine Hester?"

She stopped at large black-lacquered double doors, stuck a key in the lock, and looked at him. "She's not popular around here."

"But this is her company."

Lorna smiled slightly. "And yours too."

She opened the door, and he held it open, insisting she enter first. The 360-degree tinted-glass walls displayed awesome views of the city.

Lorna lifted a cover off a control panel on the large mahogany desk and put her finger on a button. "The walls and ceiling are heat- and light-controlled, and watch this."

She pushed the button, and a theater-sized television unfolded and rolled down from the ceiling as a black panel ran across it, blocking the sky view.

Next, the windows tinted into their black hue, and the TV started playing an AMTA "Best Talent Agency in the World" promotional loop.

When Zach turned to face her, she was holding out the keys. "Yours if you want it."

He leaned away from them. "Did Elaine turn down this office?"

"She'd rather have Archie's old office." Lorna's lips were pressed into what looked like a permanent frown.

"But did you let her know this office was available?"

"No, but she wouldn't want it." Lorna sounded sure of her claim.

"Everything smells new in here. Does she know it exists?"

She sighed heavily. "We were also going to use it as a meeting office for A-list clients. The agents seem to agree on that."

She withdrew the keys.

Zach held his hand out. "I'll take those. And no one uses this office. Got it?"

He could feel the rigidity emanating from her. After a moment, she handed him the keys, and he took them.

"By the way, I saw Allison Johnson around here

earlier. Do you have any idea why she was in the building?"

She frowned. "Allison Johnson?"

"She's an investor with Blue Star Capital."

"Oh, an investor," she said. "Investors are always in and out of here."

He shook his head. "Allison's never been interested in discretionary products. Is there a way I can find out who she came here to see?"

Lorna's eyes grew wide as he waited for her reply. She was saved by a knock at the door.

"We're in here!" she said loudly.

In walked two security guards. "Ms. Kelsey, we're here to escort you out of the building."

She scoffed bitterly then narrowed her eyes at Zach. "She's going to get what's coming to her. She's going to get it."

"Ma'am, it's time to go," one of the burly guards said.

"You know my name, Ernest."

Ernest didn't change his stern expression.

She walked toward the guards. "I knew my time was coming soon. She's a real bitch." She curled her shoulder away from Ernest. "Don't touch me."

Zach could hardly believe what was happening. He stared beyond the open doors long after Lorna and the guards had left. His mind was racing. Elaine wasn't popular, that was for sure. He could guess that although Lorna had said she knew her time was coming, she hadn't actually believed it. And what she'd said clued Zach in that there must've been a lot of firings at Elaine's hand, which was why Allison was sniffing around. He'd seen it dozens of times. A new owner came in with a heavy hand. People got unhappy. Sabotage happened. In walked someone like Allison to take advantage of the situation. And if Allison was already littering the hallways and Elaine's office, then the end was near.

Zach took his cell phone out of his pants pocket and sent Allison a text. They wouldn't meet at her hotel. He didn't want to give her the wrong impression. When it came to women, he could focus on only one at a time. It was just how he was built. At that very moment, Elaine Hester was the only woman he couldn't get out of his mind.

AN ELLIE GROSSMAN HAD REPLACED LORNA, AND she was really good at what she did because even though they both were new, she hadn't missed a beat. Zach got all he needed, including an office next to Elaine's, at least for the time being. He had plans.

He journeyed down to the twenty-third floor to speak to Cesar Martinez, the guy in charge of operations. Cesar gave him the full rundown on the sky-view office Lorna had offered Zach. Archie Rubenstein had it built for himself. After Archie was arrested, Cesar was surprised the project continued.

"It was a lot of money, and we all know the company doesn't have it. We didn't even get our bonuses last year. And now the guy's building an office. Between you and me, I'm glad he's gone."

"But who ordered construction to continue?" Zach asked.

Cesar gazed off as he shook his head. "I don't know. That's the thing—they kept it out of our department. But that didn't stop them from telling us to do this or that. None of it came out of our budget, and they would reimburse the department for man hours or equipment we gave them."

"What about the paper trail for the reimbursements?" Zach asked.

"Finance handles that. We just see the funds in our budget. That's it. No names, no nothing."

"Humph," Zach said, rubbing his chin thoughtfully.

His mind raced back to the sight of Butch's mausoleum. The sky-view office had a purpose—to show that a king was building his throne. But Lorna had tried to give him the office, and that might have been a clue that the emperor had been dethroned. Zach would know more after he had drinks with Allison later.

Cesar's crew got to work preparing the office next to Elaine's for Zach and his executive assistants. Granted, it was rough around the office that day. Elaine had fired not only Lorna but also heads of other departments, including the VP of Human Resources along with the directors and VPs of Finance and Accounting, Legal, and Information Technology. She hadn't fired most of their assistants, though. Instead, she sent out a company-wide email saying all displaced assistants would be reinterviewed and reassigned within the next five business days and the base pay for each assistant hired by the company would be seventeen dollars an hour.

She was also revamping the agents' trainee program and said they would be asking the most qualified employees if they would like to join. She left all creative sectors intact.

Paying the assistants more was an interesting decision she had made, especially in the midst of so many dismissals. Zach wondered what her strategy was and wanted to ask, but as soon as Megan and Julie arrived, he found himself locked in back-to-back conference calls that lasted late into the day.

At 6:37 p.m., he ended his last call, and his assistants went home. One thing was clear—he couldn't help run AMTA while heading Mega Link. He was meeting Allison at a local restaurant for drinks at seven. As he stepped out of his office and turned toward Elaine's, he noticed that the enclosed glass area where her assistants were supposed to sit was dim and empty. Zach leaned back so he could get a better view of Elaine's office door. Bright light seeped from the bottom of it. She was still there. He wanted desperately to walk over and say goodbye. But all it took was a single look at Elaine Hester to cloud his judgment even further. Zach knew exactly what he had to do, so he walked away from Elaine for the evening.

He arrived at the restaurant and saw Allison already sitting at the bar. She'd changed her outfit. Her long legs were crossed, and she was wearing skintight jeans and a sleeveless shirt so sheer that he could see her nipples outlined through the material. She wore high heels, her long hair was flowing, and she smelled like freshly cut flowers. Zach received her message loud and clear. She was hoping to appeal to his lust.

"Just one?" the hostess asked.

He hadn't paid attention to the hostess sitting there and offered a genuine smile as an apology. "I'm meeting someone at the bar."

She smiled back. "Enjoy your drink, then."

He winked at her and started on his way.

As soon as Allison saw him, she beamed and hopped off her stool. She made sure to press her tits against him when they hugged. He couldn't blame her for trying to pull out all the stops, since that had worked on him in the past. He'd had sex with her before—three, maybe four times, perhaps a few more than that. It had been a while since he'd experienced the pleasure of a woman or paid attention to her seduction tactics. Looking sexy, smelling good, and rubbing her chest on him would've worked if it weren't for Elaine Hester. But he also wasn't going to let Allison's bells and whistles cloud his reason for being there.

"Always handsome as hell," Allison said as she climbed back onto her stool.

Zach sat beside her. "You're the one who's looking killer hot tonight," he said, knowing his compliment would make her less careful about what she said.

"Thank you," she said, running a hand through her hair.

He motioned for the bartender, who came right over, then ordered a scotch on the rocks and another of whatever Allison had been drinking.

"Trying to get me drunk and take advantage of me, aren't you?" she asked.

He chuckled. "I'm not that smooth."

She grunted, studying him dubiously. "So what's new?" she asked, still pushing her chest out.

"Work, and I was surprised to see you at AMTA this morning."

She smiled crookedly. "You're going to get straight down to business, huh?"

"Is that what you were doing this morning? Business?"

She watched him with squinted eyes as the bartender served their drinks.

"Okay," she said, releasing the tension in her body. "I'm going to answer your questions, but when business is over, you're going to sit here and catch up with me like the old friends we are."

He lifted his glass to toast to that.

She clinked her glass against his. "Yes, I was there on business."

"What kind of business?" he asked.

Allison took a drink, and he waited for her to swallow. He knew she needed a break to form her answer.

"You know AMTA has been going through a lot of changes in recent times. I have no idea how Elaine Hester bought that company without us knowing about it. Do you?"

He nodded then took a drink. "Hell yes, I know how that happened. I'm not plugged into discretionary products, and the last I checked, neither are you."

She grinned mischievously. "And there lies our misunderstanding."

Zach tilted his head slightly.

"You should check in with me more often," she said. "I've always been a good time, haven't I?"

He sat up straight and didn't crack even a hint of a smile. "Of course."

After a moment of study, she crossed her legs and leaned toward him. "The two of you seemed cozy this morning."

"We had a meeting."

"But I know you, Zach. I saw the way you kept looking at her. You like her."

Allison was fishing for information on how he truly felt about Elaine, and he wasn't going to take the bait. "You know why I was in her office, don't you?"

She narrowed her eyes. "What are you going to do with Butch's shares?"

He cracked a smile. Now they were about to get somewhere. "I don't know. Keep them, I guess."

"Ah," she said, nodding. "A talent agency? Come on, Zach. You want me to believe that shit?"

He shrugged indifferently. "I haven't made my mind up yet."

"So you're tripping over into the discretionary side as well?"

Zach paused. "I'm a partner in AMTA. And I see someone like you in my business and I'm thinking, oh hell."

She tossed her head back and laughed. "Someone like me? You make me sound like Bloody Mary."

He grimaced. "Bloody Mary?"

"You know, the demon lady who's supposed to scratch your face up if you look in the mirror and say her name three times."

"Oh," he said.

"Really? You never played Bloody Mary as a kid?"

"Why in the hell would I play that game?"

She laughed again. "Oh, Zach, I wish you were into me the way you were into that woman." She put her mouth next to his ear. "I would fuck your brains out every moment I could."

He snorted coolly, not allowing Allison's form of foreplay to get him all hot and bothered. "But really, what were you doing there?"

She grinned tightly as she watched him, nodding. He kept an expectant look on his face.

Finally, Allison pressed her hand against her chest. "I have business, and you have business. Let's keep that in mind here."

"Are our business interests at odds?" he asked.

"They used to be until your co-owner fired some people today."

"Then you're saying whatever plans you had this morning were thwarted."

Allison raised her glass to her lips. "Did you

know Elaine Hester fired sixty-seven agents in less than a month?" She took a drink.

"I didn't," he said.

"Yes. They all went to other agencies, and ninety-three percent of their clients chose to remain at AMTA due to Elaine Hester's reputation. Do you know about her reputation?"

"I'm waiting for you tell me."

She smiled briefly. "She's skirmished with a lot of agents on behalf of her clients when she used to practice law, which is why she has so many empty offices. She's losing agents but not clients, at least for now." She took a sip of her drink.

"I see," he said. "Devalue and defeat. Nifty play."

"She's made it harder to get her out today after firing the key people. I hate that she's so fucking beautiful, but I hate her even more for being smart."

For a moment, Zach visualized himself fucking Elaine so hard, so deeply that her body merged with his, then he downed his drink to get the image out of his head.

Zach motioned to the bartender and pointed at his glass. The guy nodded.

"But listen," Allison said. "Elaine Hester is a

lawyer, not an agent. They may be down, but no agent in town is willing to work for her, so they're not out. And that's all I'm going to say."

Zach stifled a burp from drinking his scotch too fast. "That was a lot."

The bartender served him another, and he quickly said thanks.

"Well…" She shrugged. "I didn't know you were staying on at AMTA, and I like you. But whoever I'm working for isn't going away."

"You're not going to tell me who it is, are you?"

"Not tonight." Then she raised a finger. "But then, who knows what I'll say when you're inside me."

Zach laughed. "It's not you, it's me."

She laughed so hard and so suddenly that she put her hand over her mouth to keep her drink from spewing. Once she calmed herself, she pointed at him. "Don't you think I've heard that before, because I haven't."

He grinned from ear to ear. "I presumed you've heard it all."

She winked at him then raised her glass to her lips. "So… Butch is dead, huh?"

Zach knew it was time to fulfill his promise and

have a good old-fashioned friendly conversation with her. "Yep."

"Dirty old bastard."

Zach roared with laughter. Finally, someone had said it out loud. He was a dirty old bastard, always involved in dirty business too.

"You know I'm right," she said.

"Oh, I know you're right."

Then they talked about more business because they couldn't help themselves, just not that of AMTA.

CHAPTER 4

*E*laine couldn't forget the way Zach had looked at her in passing earlier that day. He'd appeared disappointed in her decision to fire so many people at once. It took her a while, but she had identified those who were plotting against her. All the new hires were from the former LH Realty. When Lord and Lord Enterprises took over, they didn't absorb the finance and accounting and human resources departments. So Elaine decided to take a chance and employ those who had found themselves out of a job. A real estate firm and a talent agency were like apples and oranges, but numbers were numbers, people were people, and she needed to trust both in order to stop losing money on her premium investment.

Money talked. The fact that she couldn't get any new agents to work for her had a lot to do with personal vendettas, but the fact she was running out of cash was also a reason. However, truth be told, she hardly ever met an agent she liked. It was as though being an asshole was a prerequisite for the job. So last week she'd had an idea, only she couldn't trust Lorna with it, so she told Ellie Grossman, her new vice president, and Lucy Chang, her new director of HR. Starting as soon as tomorrow morning, a Friday, the agent trainee program would be revamped and turned into an intensive experience. The strongest members would advance as associate agents, working closely with the eighty-nine remaining agents in the company. Elaine thought her plan was brilliant. The newer agents might not have all the contacts of an established agent, but she knew just about everyone in the entertainment business, and she was respected. In the end, she would crush her enemies, and that should've made her happy, but it didn't.

Before leaving the office, Elaine had gotten a call from her cousin Robin inviting her to dinner with Robin and another cousin, Theresa, at Craft, a nearby restaurant. Normally after a grueling day like today, she would go straight home and take a hot bath to decompress before going to bed. But she wanted to know what her cousins thought about the possibility of her entering a new relationship after what had happened with her last boyfriend, Gary. Something inside of Elaine changed forever after he double-crossed her the way he did. Gary owned a nightclub in West Hollywood and had been sleeping with one of the barely out of high school go-go dancers who worked for him. The girl he was banging was paid a lot of money to convince Gary to entice Elaine into buying AMTA. When Elaine had confronted her ex, he'd said he never suspected he was being set up. Elaine didn't believe him. There was no way he could believe a go-go dancer had a genuine line on a multibillion-dollar industry deal. If he had told her the truth about where he'd received the information regarding the sale of AMTA, she would've known to stay away from it. She would have broken up with him before wasting billions of dollars on a company that had been overpriced and a headache from day two.

When Elaine arrived at the restaurant, Robin and Theresa were already seated. Not long after she sat down, the waitress came over to take their order. Elaine didn't need to look at the menu since the restaurant was one of her favorite spots. She didn't usually like to drink alcohol when her stomach was empty, but she ordered a dry white wine, anyway.

"You look beat," Theresa said.

Elaine turned to see her cousin looking her over as though she were a car wreck. "I'm fine," she lied.

"Really? Is that your story and you're sticking to it?" Robin asked.

"Ease up, okay?" Elaine snapped.

Theresa and Robin stared incredulously at each other.

Elaine sighed. Of course they were able to see right through her. Every moment of the day had been leading her closer to her breaking point. Her carefully crafted facade was becoming more like a moth-eaten cloak.

"Okay, something's wrong," she confessed.

"Then let's lay it on the table and deal with it," Theresa said. That was the Hester-women way.

Lots of people who worked for or knew Elaine frequented the restaurant, so she looked over one side of her shoulder then the other and did a double take. A familiar pair of eyes were watching her. Her heart pounded like thunder. Zach was turned in their direction while Allison was facing the bar. They didn't look as cozy as she'd imagined they would. Then he smirked at her, and she quickly faced forward.

"Who's that?" Theresa asked.

"Who's who?" Elaine replied.

Theresa pointed at Zach. "That guy right there."

Elaine felt her eyes widen with horror. Theresa was gazing at him as if they were visiting a zoo and he were a caged unicorn. She leaned toward her shameless cousin. "Stop it," she hissed.

"Stop what?" She was still gazing at him.

"Staring."

"Who is he, though?"

It was time to lie. "I don't know."

"Okay, whatever, but you're supposed to tell us why you look like death warmed over," Robin said.

Elaine clutched her stomach, which was turning a little. "Because AMTA is still giving me hell."

"Then get rid of it."

Elaine closed her eyes and muttered, "If only it were that easy."

"I agree. That would be a lot of wasted money," Theresa said.

"You can't put a price tag on happiness," Robin said. "I know it sounds cliché, but it's true."

Thank goodness the server arrived with their

first course, salads. Theresa's cell phone buzzed, distracting her even more. Elaine was starving, so as soon as the waiter left, she dug right in. They all did.

"Anyway, I have another announcement," Theresa said as she stuffed her phone, which was on the table at first, into her purse. Apparently, she had been waiting for whoever had just texted to contact her.

"We're listening," Elaine said, glad the spotlight was off her even though she was really giving Robin's comments a lot of thought.

"I'm moving to Seattle. I mean, sure, you backed out on our business deal," she told Elaine. "And I was upset about that, but maybe it was fate because the Seattle Settlers just offered me the job as their coordination trainer."

"Coordination trainer? What the hell is that?" Elaine asked.

"Doesn't sound important enough for you?" Theresa crammed a forkful of avocado into her mouth.

Elaine felt her grimace linger. That hurt. She always wanted the best for her cousins and sister. They knew that. It was what she thought Gran expected of them. After she bailed her mother out of jail and paid to make the charges go away the last time, she had asked herself why she did that. Why was she always meddling in the lives of everyone she loved or was supposed to love? When Theresa complained about the woman she was partnering with to open a high-tech advanced fitness center in Seattle, Elaine figured she would give her cousin enough money to be rid of her difficult colleague so that she could make all the decisions on her own. Two months later, however, Theresa changed her mind about the fitness center. When Elaine had asked why, she'd said, "My heart isn't in it."

Surprisingly, Elaine didn't blow up and accuse her of being wishy-washy and noncommittal or a self-saboteur. She had no idea why she hadn't said those things, because she certainly felt them, but perhaps it was because she felt her opinion of her cousin was more habit than the deep humanizing truth. Something was off inside, so a few weeks later, Elaine bought AMTA to prove she was just fine.

Elaine watched Theresa's eyes almost daring her to be critical. She pasted a smile on her face. "As long as your decision is important to you, that's all that matters."

Theresa grunted. "Was that a carefully crafted insult?"

"No," Elaine and Robin said at the same time.

She was surprised Robin was taking her side on this. That rarely happened.

"Listen, I don't know what's right for you"—she pointed at Robin—"or you. Hell, it seems as though I don't know what's right for myself anymore."

She clamped her lips together, but from their expressions, it appeared her cousins were expecting her to elaborate.

Elaine rubbed the back of her neck. "Um…" She readjusted in her seat.

"Sorry, but did you just say 'um'?" Theresa asked.

"Ladies," a man said.

They all quickly turned and saw Zach standing at the edge of their table. Elaine felt her eyes grow wide. She wanted to bail out. And the way he smiled as his eyes landed on all the faces at the table before settling on hers made her heart nearly thump out of her chest.

He put a hand on Elaine's back. "Elaine, didn't mean to startle you, just wanted to say good night before I head home."

They were staring into each other's eyes again. For a moment, she felt as though it were her duty to introduce him to her family as her new love interest. But then she remembered that falling for him would spell trouble for her. She also remembered he was not alone and searched to his left and right to see whether his date was lurking. She wasn't. "Where's Allison?"

His smirk was back. "I don't know where she is."

She wanted to ask whether Allison was on her way to his house for a nightcap but decided it wasn't appropriate. Plus, what if he said he was planning to join Allison later? Then Elaine would have to deal with heartbreak all over again.

"Laney, have you turned red?" Theresa asked, grinning from ear to ear.

"Huh?" Elaine hoped not. She didn't need Zach Lord seeing the effect he had on her.

"By the way, I'm Zach Lord."

Theresa half stood to shake his hand. "I'm Theresa." She pointed at Robin. "And that's my sister, Robin."

Robin shook his hand.

It fell awkwardly silent for a few beats.

"So Zach, how do you and Laney know each

other?" Theresa asked, her eyes shining with obvious amusement.

He tilted his head slightly. "Laney?"

"It's short for Elaine," Theresa said.

Zach flexed his eyebrows. "I like it."

"Excuse me, but are you related to Jack Lord?" Robin asked.

Elaine was surprised Robin had asked that. Perhaps it was because she had spent a few days in New York with Elaine's sister, Sonja, who was becoming fast friends with Daisy, Jack Lord's wife.

"Related but distantly."

"Humph." She pursed her lips into an obligatory smile.

"How do you know each other again?"

"So yes"—Elaine shot to her feet—"these are my cousins. We were just having dinner."

Their faces were so close that she had to struggle against the natural inclination to kiss him.

"Would you like to join us?" Theresa asked.

Elaine felt her eyes expand in sheer horror as the future played out in her mind. Theresa would be flirting with him all night, which would've been another clue that her picker was off, because Terri's picker was even worse than hers. Robin would subtly interrogate him, asking all sorts of questions —ranging from his worldview to his deepest, darkest secrets—without being aware that she was doing it.

"But how do you two know each other?" Robin asked, shifting her pointed finger between Elaine and Zach.

"We're business partners," Elaine replied while still trapped in Zach's gaze.

"Business partners? How?

Finally, Elaine ripped her eyes off Zach and turned to her cousins, who were watching her curiously. "Remember those thirty-nine shares owned by Butch Benjamin?"

"Yes," they said in unison.

"Butch died two days ago, and now Zach here, his nephew, is in charge of those shares."

"Oh," Robin and Theresa said, again at the same time.

The server arrived at the table with their main courses, and Zach took a step back to let him take the edge.

"Well, didn't mean to interrupt your dinner," he said.

"No, really. Sit. Join us," Theresa said, watching him with stars in her eyes.

He put his hands up. "I would love to, but I can't tonight."

Elaine wanted to lay into him for planning to traipse off and bang Allison later, but then that would've made her look crazy, and on most days she wasn't one of those crazy, irrational women.

"It was nice meeting you, Zach," Robin said.

"I hope we meet again," Theresa said, which made Robin roll her eyes.

"You ladies have a nice evening." Zach put a hand on the small of Elaine's back, causing that spot to tingle. "I'll see you in the morning."

Elaine could hardly breathe after he kissed her on the cheek and walked away. She wasn't expecting that. Why did he do that?

Her eyes remained stuck on his backside until he found her face just before he walked out the door and winked at her.

"Whoa, Laney," Robin said.

"Huh?" She was flustered and couldn't hide it.

"You like him."

Elaine sat down and straightened her back. "No. I can't like him."

"Why not?" Theresa asked.

She allowed the server to finish delivering their

meals. The guy smiled flirtatiously at Elaine before asking if they needed anything else.

"We're fine," Robin said impatiently. It was clear she wanted to interrogate Elaine about her feelings for Zach.

"No, thank you," Theresa said briskly.

The server walked away.

"So why can't you like him?" Robin asked again once they were alone.

"Because of Gary, Peter, Todd, and Russell and an assortment of other bad boyfriends."

"I think—" Theresa said.

"But he's not like those guys," Robin said, cutting her sister off. "Zach Lord seems different from *your* average Joe."

Elaine stopped slicing into her scallop. "I know." She knew she sounded sad about it.

Robin frowned at her. "But it's good for you. Your insecurity chose those other guys. You had no hesitation when it came to starting a relationship with those guys. I believe Zach Lord makes you diffident. And in your case, that's a breakthrough."

Theresa broke out into a laugh. "Don't you just love it," she said and pointed her fork at Robin. "Now that, my friend, is how you do a carefully crafted insult."

"I'm not insulting her." Robin's gaze caressed Elaine's face. "I'm not insulting you, Laney. I'm proud of you. Yes, don't be afraid to give the guy a chance. He likes you."

"No, that was an insult. I didn't say it wasn't true, but damn, Robbie, the way you do that is just as artful as your art."

Robin rolled her eyes while shaking her head.

"Don't anyone put me up under Zach Lord too soon. He is Butch Benjamin's nephew. And he does want my company."

"Carrie Ann's your mom, and Lily Rose is ours. None of us are anything like them. So it's not fair to assume he and Butch Benjamin have similar characters."

Theresa shook her fork at Robin. "Now that's true. The last I talked to our mom, she was on her sixth marriage to a guy who was older than King Tut's mummy."

Elaine snorted. For some reason, her aunt Lily Rose liked old, old guys, and being rich was not mandatory. They only had to be ancient. "Now that's old."

"I know. It's embarrassing."

Silence fell between them. The topic of their mothers was generally depressing.

"Well," Robin said, changing the subject, "I also have an announcement."

Both Elaine and Theresa looked at her with curious frowns.

"I'm hitting the road starting next week."

"Hit the road? What the hell does that mean?" Theresa asked.

Robin said she had just finished an art installation project and then explained how she'd captured the many forms of light and sound and used particles to materialize them both.

"Sonja put me in touch with a woman named Claudia Francois, and she landed me a few exhibitions in Germany, England, Switzerland, Tokyo, and Toronto."

"That's more than a few," Elaine said.

Robin shrugged, but Elaine could see she was nervous about her new decision from the way she looked down at her plate when she said, "I guess so."

"So you're leaving LA?" Theresa asked.

"For a while, yes. Maybe forever, I don't know."

"First Sonja, then me, and now you. Oh and Gran…" Theresa turned to Elaine. "That leaves you here all by yourself, Laney." She sounded sad.

Elaine turned to look at Theresa, who had

watery eyes. Elaine wrapped an arm gently around her cousin's neck, guided her near, and kissed her on the cheek. "That's why they make planes, trains, and automobiles."

"No matter what, we still have to have our monthly dinners," Theresa said.

"Agreed," Elaine said.

"Of course," Robin added.

They all knew they were merely deluding themselves. Their lives would become remarkably busy, and one month would turn into the next, and many days would go by before they actually spent time at the table with each other again.

"Don't you guys feel it?" Theresa asked.

"I feel it," Robin said.

"Everything's about to change."

They all sat in silence long enough to let the sadness pass. Then Theresa started describing the cute house she'd bought, nestled on the shores of the bay in Seattle. One subject turned into the next, and thank goodness Elaine didn't give Zach Lord another thought.

CHAPTER 5

*A*t least, she didn't give him another thought until she got home after dinner. Elaine's body recalled all the times Zach Lord had stood close to her that day. It wasn't just the way he looked, either—she liked him.

Zach had a certain elegance most men didn't possess. That was probably why, after only one brief meeting, Robin had a lot of faith in him. Her cousin was a good judge of character, but Elaine had a lot to lose if he wasn't what she thought he was.

She recalled the three billion she'd spent to buy a company that was barely worth one of those billions. She had earned that money from a gamble made by investing in a little-known company called ConnectUp six years ago. Two years after she used all of her salary surplus to purchase $2.7 million worth of shares, the company had become the largest social media platform on the planet. It was a gamble she'd been banking on losing. She'd never wanted to be wealthy. Elaine would've always settled for a good husband who was the rich and powerful one. But the only men she knew like that were controlling dicks who preferred overly made-up Bratz dolls. She tried being that girl, once or twice, when she was in college. The problem was, the guy had to be smarter than her to make it work, and that was rarely the case.

But was Zach Lord that guy? She doubted it. She bet he was a masterful charmer and then, once he'd trapped his prey, wham, their head would be sliced clean off. Yep, that was him. For sure it was him.

By the time Elaine had decided to remain leery of the suave, sexy, and charming billionaire, she was ready to turn off the late news, which she hadn't absorbed even a second of, and fall asleep. Then her cell phone rang. It was her sister, Sonja, calling from New York.

"It's late here, but it's super early there. What's

going on?" Elaine asked as soon as she answered the call.

"Jay and I did it. Four days ago, we went to the courthouse and tied the knot. We're in Phuket now, but we're flying back to New York later today."

Elaine flung her body forward to sit in an upright position. "You're married?"

"We decided to just do it. Why wait? We're both adults, and neither of us are into the marriage ceremony hoopla."

"Hoopla?" Elaine repeated as though it were a dirty word.

Sonja sighed hard. "I thought you'd be happy."

Elaine could hardly believe Sonja had said that. If her sister knew even a little bit about her, then she would've known not even a morsel of her would be happy to hear that she and Jay had eloped. And Sonja had known enough about Elaine to write a book about her.

"And why in the hell did you think that, Sonja? You know what, you're selfish. Always have been, always will be."

Sonja fell silent. Elaine knew her sister was just allowing her to ponder the horrible words she had just spoken. What she had said was mean, but shit, Sonja was wrong, so very wrong, for robbing her of a ceremony that would actually end with two people pronounced man and wife.

Elaine closed her eyes to stop the tears from falling. "I'm sorry, Son."

"Apology accepted."

"It's just…"

Sonja sighed. "Laney, you love me, don't you?"

"You know that I do."

"And Jay, you love him too?"

"Of course. Why are you asking me these silly questions?"

"We just went to the courthouse because our hearts and minds were already partners for life. So there's no reason to have a bloated, time-consuming ceremony. If you need us to show up like that, then let's have a big family dinner to commemorate our nuptials next month sometime. How about that?"

Elaine jerked her head. "If *I*?"

"Well, yes, you."

She felt heat flushing through her body. "Don't spin this, little sister. You fucked up. Because all that yarn you were spinning about love and partners in the heart is the only reason to have a marriage ceremony. And Gran was very excited about seeing the two of you exchange vows. So you know what? Forget all that BS I just heard and, instead of a dinner, have a fucking wedding next month! Even if you have to do it twice. Good night." She ended their call and threw her phone on the chaise in the corner of her room.

At first she couldn't fall asleep for thinking about Zach, but now it was Sonja occupying too much space in her head. Elaine hated that Sonja was now the only Hester girl who was married. She should've been first. When it came to her sister and cousins, Elaine had done everything first—first kiss, first to have sex, first to graduate from college and law school, first to buy a multimillion-dollar mansion, and first to be proposed to, all four times.

Regardless, at some point in the wee hours of the morning, Elaine had finally fallen asleep. But not long afterward, the alarm on her cell phone had chimed, and she jumped out of bed and ran over to the chaise to turn it off. First, she checked to see if Sonja had called her back. She hadn't. Elaine didn't know whether that was a good or bad sign. Then she did something that she'd been doing quite often lately—she sat on the foot of the bed, her shoulders slumped, wailing.

"Why am I crying?" she whispered, wiping her eyes with the backs of her hands.

There wasn't just one clearly identifiable reason

she was sobbing. There were many, and they were all buried way too deep beneath the surface for her to do anything about them. If she had resolved her sadness, then everything would change. She wasn't ready for that, not yet at least.

"Zach," she whispered.

He would be her first meeting of the morning. She didn't want to admit to herself that he was the reason she mustered the energy to get up, put on a suit that fit her like a glove, pretty her face, make sure she smelled divine, and head to the office.

But still, Elaine remained in a fog as she drove to work. After arriving, she sat in the silence of her special parking space reserved just for her and gripped the steering wheel while crying some more. Going on a crying jag in the parking lot was also something she'd been doing a lot lately.

Tap, tap, tap.

Elaine jumped, and her hand flew to her chest as she turned toward the driver's window. Zach's face was in line with hers.

"Are you okay?" he asked.

"Shit," she muttered and reached for a tissue. "I'm fine. See you inside." Before blowing her nose, she turned and waited for him to walk away. Zach just stood there.

She pasted on a smile. "You can leave. I'm fine."

He took a step back. "I'll wait."

She turned on the power to her car and rolled down the window. "No. Leave."

Zach folded his arms. "Elaine, I'm not leaving, so get out of the car."

What a dick! She was convinced he wanted to see her humiliated and weak. Perhaps there was no time better than the present to go for the kill. She was more determined than ever to show him her strength. Elaine blew her nose, patted her face dry so as not to disturb her makeup, grabbed her purse, and calm, cool, and collected, she got out of the car.

Her back straight and her head held high, she looked him in the eyes. "In the future, when I ask for privacy, give it to me."

"I'm not your enemy," he said so sincerely that, for a moment, she felt as if she could believe him.

They stared into each other's eyes. The mere act made Elaine want to cry again, but she fought like hell to avoid it.

"Elaine." He smiled slightly. "Laney."

She felt her eyes brighten.

"I have a proposition for you."

Now she frowned.

"I agree with you about your thirty-nine shares. With the price you paid for the company, you should own it fully, outright. So I'm going to give you your shares."

Her head felt as though it were floating way above her shoulders. Had she heard what she thought she'd heard? Was Zachary Lord going to so easily give her what she wanted? *Do I want them?*

She cleared the lump from her throat. "Thank you."

"But first you have to come with me."

Elaine rolled her eyes and crossed her arms like a petulant child. "Of course—you're bullshitting me."

He shook his head. "I'm not bullshitting you. I will give you your shares if you spend the day with me. But I lead, you follow, no questions asked."

She grimaced. "You lead? What the hell does that mean?"

"It's not a riddle. You do what I say for one day, and I'll give you your share."

She threw her hands up, her palms facing him. "Is this like some sexual BDSM bullshit? Because I'm not into that and never will be."

Zach smirked. "Neither am I. But I want to

show you some things that'll help you. I'll never hurt you."

Elaine narrowed her eyes as she pondered his proposition. Could she win so easily? Never. "Can I get that in writing?"

"I would say yes, but no. You're going to have to trust me."

Her mouth fell open, and he raised a hand.

"I know this is hard for you, but like I said, you spend the day with me, or two days, and you'll get your shares back."

She slightly tilted her head. "You said I have to spend one day with you."

"Thirty-nine shares, two days. Or three. I think that's fair."

She rolled her eyes as she shook her head. "You're already being dishonest."

He stepped closer. "Okay, one day for sure. By day two, I will take you home but only if you ask. On day three…" He winked while displaying the sort of grin that made women want to drop their panties.

Elaine couldn't recall how to think, but suddenly she remembered to breathe. "You promise?"

He put his hand over his heart. "I promise."

CHAPTER 6

Zach wouldn't tell Elaine where they were going, only that he had business to take care of today, and it wasn't in LA. He had allowed her to call Fiona Meadows, vice president of the company, to let her know she would be out for the day.

"Oh no, are you sick?" Fiona had asked.

"No. Just busy."

"Busy with what? We're supposed to be busy here today."

Elaine nodded. "I know… But I'm with Zach Lord today, and we're hammering out a deal to get my shares back." She peeked at him, and he was sneering.

Fiona took a long pause. "Okay, then. See you Monday."

Elaine climbed up into the passenger seat of Zach's humongous SUV. It felt strange being alone with a man she was severely attracted to. They were already going west on Olympic Boulevard when she realized there was no music wailing out of the speakers. "You don't listen to music?" she asked.

"Feel free to listen to whatever you like. I have satellite radio." He reached for the knob.

She quickly put her hand on top of his to stop him from turning on the radio. "I didn't say that I wanted to listen to music. I asked if you listened to it."

He removed his hand without turning on the radio. "Oh. No. I'd rather hear my thoughts when I'm driving."

Elaine settled against her seat. "Me too." She was happy they had that in common.

"I like music, though," he said. "Just not in the car."

"Same here." Elaine closed her eyes. She didn't want to feel so relaxed but couldn't help it. "It's just that every single time I get into a man's car, he has some awful song blasting. I'm particularly annoyed by the driver's-seat deejay."

He laughed.

"Switching from one song to the next, to the next, to the next." She shook her head. "Annoying."

Zach laughed harder. "You know the guy was only trying to impress you."

She opened her eyes. "No way."

"Of course. It was his way of showing off. He wanted you to know who he was through his music. That's all."

Elaine grimaced as she thought back on one ex who'd had the worst case of driver's-seat disc jockeying. He played a lot of New Age instrumentals. Every song was like musical gymnastics, notes jumping from here to there and everywhere, roving all over the place, just as his eyes would every time they were out together and another attractive woman passed by.

"What's on your mind?" Zach asked.

Elaine raised her eyebrows. "I was just thinking about someone."

"In regard to what we're talking about?"

She glanced at him. That was another thing she liked about Zach—he was a clear communicator. "Yeah. But it wasn't a good memory."

He didn't say anything, but she kept her eyes on

the road. Then she knew exactly where they were going.

"Are you taking me to the airport?" she asked in shock.

"Remember our deal?"

"Okay, but can't I ask you if we're catching a flight to somewhere?"

"No, you may not, but the answer to your question is yes."

She sniffed. "This is ridiculous, Zach. You said spend the day with you, and I'll do that, but you can at least tell me where we're going."

He rubbed his chin thoughtfully. "Yes, I can. But I won't."

"Will I be safe? I can ask that, can't I?"

"What did I tell you?"

She frowned, confused.

"I would never harm you. You believed me then, and I know you still do. Just relax, Laney, and enjoy the day."

When he called her "Laney," it was as though he had been calling her that all of her life. So Elaine folded her arms and tried to do what he said. It was difficult, though. Then she remembered something.

"So how did your get-together with Allison go?"

"I was going to debrief you when we get on the airplane."

"I can ask you a question about that, can't I? It has nothing to do with our trip, or does it?"

He cut a tiny smile. "It doesn't. But I wanted to have a longer, uninterrupted conversation with you about what she and I talked about and offer some suggestions, if you want to take them."

"Sure, I'll hear your suggestions," she said. That was a no-brainer. Zach was an effective venture capitalist. She had been trained to acquire and utilize sound advice when it came to business.

He looked at her and did a double take. "Thanks."

"You're welcome."

It fell quiet again, but the sexual tension in the air was pretty loud. Spending one whole day with Zach Lord was not going to be easy.

"So, Elaine," he said, "are you going to tell me why you were crying?"

She opened her mouth to tell him the honest truth. She didn't know why. But then maybe he would think she was depressed or something. She wanted to lie but couldn't. "I don't know why," she said, taking a chance on the truth.

"Can I ask you something?"

"Apparently. You're the one calling the shots, for now."

"I am, aren't I?" He sounded happy about it.

She rolled her eyes and sighed hard.

He laughed. "Okay, here's what I want to know."

Zach had her complete attention.

"What makes you happy?"

Elaine looked stunned, because she'd never pondered that question, and no one had ever asked her, not even Robin, who would so ask that sort of thing. Then she wondered why. Why hadn't her deep and emotionally intelligent cousin ever asked what made her happy? Perhaps because the truth was one of those devastating things about her that lived far beneath the surface but showed itself in some sort of negative trait that Robin thought best to let her have and hold. Her cousin was always paying attention to the shit no one ever acknowledged about themselves.

"Why don't you think about it and get back to me later," he said.

"Are you requiring an answer?"

"No. I'm not. I'd just like to learn more about you."

She could sense that he wasn't being patronizing.

Elaine snuck a look at him and said, "I'll think about it."

"I'll be waiting to hear it."

When she glanced at him again, he was already watching her with a grin.

THEY HAD MADE IT TO LAX, AND ZACH WAS chartering a plane to somewhere. It felt so ridiculous to go with the program. Who ever hopped on an airplane without knowing where they were going unless they were being kidnapped? Was he kidnapping her? Elaine didn't have to ask him that question. She already knew the answer—of course not. Perhaps there was something to him insisting on taking charge. She hated giving up her power.

Elaine had walked up the ramp and strapped herself into a reclining leather chair when the sad answer to Zach's earlier question came to her.

"Zach," she said quietly.

He was sitting across from her, and his eyes let her know that she had his complete attention.

"It's power."

"What's power?"

"What I've always loved. Power."

She felt so choked up as he studied her.

"At least that's what you think."

She shook her head fervently. "It's what I know."

"I don't think you've discovered what you love, at least not yet."

Why wouldn't he listen to her? What was he talking about? Never had Elaine felt so emotionally stilted. Thank goodness his cell phone rang, which allowed her to silently gaze out the window and regret what she'd just told him. But she at least learned by listening to him that they were on their way to New York so he could assess a future business venture, and the second call was from his mother. He hadn't revealed much when speaking to her, other than repeating numerous times that he understood how she felt, then ending the call by saying, "Love you" and "See you soon."

Elaine quickly turned to look at him as the airplane headed toward the runway for takeoff.

"You're not taking me to visit your mother, are you?"

"Was that a question you just asked, because how many times do I have to remind you—"

"I know," she said, not wanting to hear the rules of their little adventure one more time.

Soon, they were darting down the runway, and the flight attendant was serving breakfast. Elaine hadn't realized how hungry she was until digging into the whole-grain blueberry pancakes, turkey bacon, and scrambled eggs. At least it felt like business again as Zach finally told her about his meeting with Allison.

He said she was at the company because AMTA was vulnerable to a takeover. Elaine had fired all the right people yesterday, which caused major setbacks in the plan of whoever wanted to snatch the company out of her hands. For the sake of future business and to protect her clients, Allison wouldn't reveal their names. However, she strongly believed Elaine would eventually run the business into the ground, and Allison's clients would have another shot at owning the agency.

"Why is that?" Elaine asked, feeling the insult come down on her like a jackhammer.

"I think she believes your agents are going to sabotage you."

Then Elaine explained her new agent-training program to him. Zach watched her intensely until he shifted abruptly in his seat.

"What are you thinking?" she asked, recognizing he had a whole different way of viewing her brilliant plan.

"Aren't you a lawyer?" he asked.

"Yes." Her tone asked him to explain his question.

"You're not an agent."

"And?" She took offense.

He threw up his hands. "If you can't recognize or appreciate someone else's profession, then you're fucked. You can't wear all hats, because you don't."

Elaine felt his words trying to penetrate her thick skull. She wanted to absorb them but was finding it difficult.

"What do they do? Put packets together? Get their clients jobs? They make it harder than it should be with their backbiting and manipulating. They're the worst bandits in the world!" She nudged herself in the chest as she said, "I'm having none of that in my company. Those who want to be burglars can do it somewhere else."

He leaned forward. "Did you just say 'burglars'?"

"Yes, because that's what they are."

Zach sat back in his seat and grunted. His coolness made her feel like an idiot for becoming impassioned over the subject of talent agents.

"Can I ask you something?"

She shrugged.

"Why did you choose to own a talent agency if you have animosity toward the workers who determine whether you sink or swim?"

Elaine was about to blow up and say she was the one who determined whether she survived, but then she remembered something Robin once said to her. She had said that perhaps Elaine should think about *why* she was flying off the handle *when* she was flying off the handle.

"Okay, let me ask you something else," he said.

Elaine shifted uncomfortably in her seat. "What?"

"Have you ever put together packages for entertainment products?"

He sounded all business, and even though Elaine felt defensive, she couldn't ignore how attractive he was.

"Yes," she said. "The last one I put together earned the highest ratings to date for a show on the AEE network." She raised a finger. "And my sister and my new brother-in-law, who both, by the way, ran off and got—" She stopped and took a breath. Holy hell, what in the world was wrong with her?

"Your sister?" he asked in a quiet voice.

Elaine closed her eyes. All she wanted was for their day to be over with already. She didn't want to talk about Sonja and Jay or how jealous she was about them being married. She was sure that hearing the news from Sonja last night was what had screwed with her sleep. She knew her sister's engagement wouldn't end as all four of hers had, and perhaps that was the reason Elaine had cried so much recently.

"It's nothing."

"It doesn't look like nothing from where I'm sitting."

She opened her eyes and willed the tears to stay put. "My sister eloped, that's all."

"And that makes you unhappy?" he said, as though he knew there was more to what she was feeling.

"Maybe. I don't know."

"But you do know."

Elaine wanted to run her hand nervously through her hair, but she had her strands tied in a tight, neat bun. She rubbed the back of her neck instead.

"What are you, like, a therapist or something?"

He chuckled. "Nope. I'm a no bullshitter. I don't bullshit myself or others. For instance, I like you, Elaine. I've been wanting to kiss you ever since yesterday. Last night, I wanted to sit and have dinner with you and your cousins, but being around you makes me nervous, although your presence is the only place I want to be these days, and that scares the shit out of me."

Suddenly, Elaine forgot everything they had been talking about before his confession. Her head felt light, and her heart was quickly pounding. No man had ever been bold enough to sit right in front of her and speak those words. For that, she admired him. But she still couldn't trust him. Instead, she wondered what sort of game Zach Lord was playing. He didn't play fair, that was for sure.

She took a deep breath. "I see."

He appeared disappointed by her businesslike tone.

"Okay," he said and pursed his lips. "Business it is. So just think about your agents, day in and day out putting together packages for entertainment products. They're negotiating for clients who are signed to your agency. And they're dealing with more than actors, directors—"

"I know what a package includes," she said as softly as she could. Elaine didn't want to change the subject or talk about his attraction to her, but she knew she had to address it. "Zach, I want to say that I'm flattered. I truly am, but I've been engaged four times," she said, holding up four fingers. "And my last fiancé is the one who tricked me into buying AMTA after being used by a go-go dancer who worked in his nightclub. He was cheating on me with her."

"Wow," he said, surprise showing on his face. "What a fucking idiot."

Elaine's mouth fell open. She could tell he meant it.

"Making love to you, your softness, your curves, your face. What the fuck was wrong with him?"

She rolled her eyes. "Well, I'm not that soft."

His gaze started at her legs then went up to her chest and finally stopped on her face. "Why do you say that?" he asked breathlessly.

His lust was already doing pleasurable things to her, so she struggled to get a grip. "Because…" She adjusted in her seat. "I'm a tough bitch."

"That's not what I discovered about you."

Elaine was holding on to a thread when it came to stopping herself from jumping his bones. Her eyes rolled down to his bulging package. He wanted her. And from what was occurring in her nether regions, she wanted him too.

"Sorry, I have to go to the restroom." She slid her tray from in front of her and started tugging at her seat belt.

His hands were on top of her knees. "Do you really have to go to the restroom?"

"Um…" Only to cool down and get control of herself.

"Are you wet?" he asked.

Her mouth was open.

"Can I see?"

She still couldn't speak.

Slowly, he parted her knees and crept her skirt up her thighs. Zach released a sporadic breath at the sight of her crotch. His finger slid up and down her drenched panties. With each stroke, a tickling sensation sparked in her pussy. She clutched the handle of the seat. Their eye contact was firm.

"Tell me to stop, and I will," he whispered.

He did it again, and she pinched the back of her head against the seat. "Stop." The word came out without her consent.

She regretted saying it as soon as his finger

stopped pleasuring her. He pulled her skirt toward her knees, and he sat back in his seat.

They were both breathing heavily as Elaine gazed at the sky through the round window. They were the only two adults in the main cabin, so they could indeed make adult decisions. All she wanted to say was "Go. Don't stop. Go." But Elaine had to remind herself what was at stake.

Oh, what a vicious game, Zach Lord.

He was playing it well.

"So, Laney…"

When she faced him, he was smirking. She quickly looked at the sky. "What?"

"Tell me about yourself. You said you were born and raised in Hollywood?"

"Hancock Park," she replied, refusing to look at that sexy grin of his.

"You seem pretty conservative to be from a city like Los Angeles."

"I've just learned my lesson, that's all."

"You've been hurt."

"More times than you know."

"Four times at least," he said.

She shrugged.

"You know, I'm really good at unpacking shit,

getting to the bottom of why you've been hurt a lot. There's always a reason."

She whipped her face around, and her scathing glare landed on him. "Me? What about you, Zach?"

"Shoot. I'm an open book."

Elaine folded her arms. "Okay, did you have sex with Allison last night?"

"No, I did not."

"Have you ever had sex with her?"

"Yes, I have."

Elaine unfolded her arms and pinched her back against the seat. She suspected he had but hadn't expected him to cop to it.

"I'm not into her, Elaine."

"But you once were."

"You were once into four men, at least. We both have pasts."

Damn it. What a great comeback.

"But Allison is lurking right here and now. Did she come on to you last night?"

He jerked his neck and said emphatically, "Of course. But like I said, I'm not into her. Listen, I'm not one of those guys who has issues focusing on one magnificent and sexy woman at a time."

"Then you're saying she's magnificent and sexy?"

He chuckled. "You are a lawyer and, I suspect, a damn good one."

Elaine cracked a smile. Perhaps her insecurity was glaring at the moment. She should definitely tone it down. "Sorry, don't answer that."

"Good, because I know what you're doing."

Her posture perked up. "And what's that?"

"If you can tell yourself that I'm into another woman, it'll make it easier for you to dismiss me. But Laney, I'm not into any woman but you."

She looked down then away. "But you just met me yesterday."

"Actually, you had left an impression on me the day before yesterday, at the cemetery."

His tone had gone flat, so she whipped her face around to look at him. He was staring down at his hands.

"You must've been pretty close to Butch for him to leave you everything."

He looked up. "We were close. But I know my uncle wasn't a saint."

"You said he was your mother's brother?"

"Yeah," he whispered and cleared his throat.

"Were they close?"

"They hadn't been in a long time."

"Why not?" Elaine was never much of a prier, not unless it had something to do with work. Her mind raced back to her last relationship. She'd never asked Gary such intimate questions about himself or his family. Hell, she didn't even know Gary's mother's name.

"Butch didn't like my father. I always suspected Butch thought my father believed he was better than him. My dad's an ethno and historical archeologist."

"Wow." Elaine nodded, impressed. "I've never met one of those before."

Zach smiled appreciatively. "He's pretty well-known. His findings and work have been covered in *National Geographic* over sixty times. He's published a lot of books, and the artifacts he's unearthed are on display in museums across the world."

Elaine smiled. "You sound proud of him."

He crossed and uncrossed his legs. "Very much so. What about your parents?"

The dreaded question. "Well, my mom is a loser, and my dad's an even bigger loser. Need I say more?"

He shook his head emphatically. "Nope."

"My grandmother raised my sister and me," she

said, because she felt like adding the redeeming part of her life story.

"Lorraine Hester?"

"Yes," she said with a smile.

"She's a remarkable woman."

"Yes, she is."

They beamed at each other.

Suddenly, Elaine remembered the warning she'd been wanting to issue to Zach. "Oh, speaking of remarkable women, I would watch out for Betsy Benjamin if I were you. Since you said you were thinking about making her trustee over Butch's assets."

She shared with him every detail of the talk she'd had with Betsy the other day.

All he said was "Humph" and then "Thank you."

Elaine didn't know what to make of his response, but at least she'd warned him. If Betsy ended up fucking a whole lot of people, at least Zach had been cautioned.

Conversation flowed easily for the rest of their flight. Zach wanted to hear all about her cousins and Sonja. He laughed at the quirks and nodded approvingly at their accomplishments. "It's clear you all love each other," he said.

"We do," she proudly proclaimed. She smiled warmly as memories of the most important women in her life danced through her head.

"Elaine?" Zach asked.

She shook herself out of her beautiful daydream to look at him.

"Can I kiss you now?"

The question took her breath away so much that all she could do was nod.

CHAPTER 7

The kissing started slowly. His warm and heavy breaths clashed with hers. Zach made her realize just how soft her lips were with each brush of his own. He had said he'd been waiting to kiss her, and she could hardly wait.

His kiss was deep, indulgent. Her head was spinning. His fingers were under the crotch of her panties, and he was rubbing her clit so steadily that her lips broke away from his so she could suck air.

"Elaine, let me," he said.

"We'll be landing in fifteen minutes," the captain said through the loudspeakers.

However, Zach hadn't stopped rubbing her clit. Elaine squeezed her eyes shut, calling out for the most high. Her hips couldn't help her escape what his fingers were doing. The sensations. Holy hell, was that what she had been pretending to feel for all those years? Goodness, had she sold herself short? Future wives didn't let prospective husbands rub their pussies while they were on airplanes, did they? All the magazines and dating experts warned not to give a man such access without a commitment. And then it happened, causing Elaine to moan and cry out louder than she ever had in her life.

WHEN THEIR BRIEF ENCOUNTER WAS OVER, THEIR fixed gazes lingered. Then he kissed her tenderly before gently guiding the hem of her skirt toward her knee and taking his seat. Elaine felt as though she should say something. If not her, then him. But Zach continued watching her without uttering a word.

She searched for the right thing to say. All she could come up with was "Wow" and "Please do it again, but this time let's go all the way." She knew better than to voice either thought out loud. The way he sat and watched her made her sink deeper into her seat.

"What?" she finally asked.

"I'm just thinking," he said.

"I can see that. What are you thinking?"

His eyebrows rose, and Elaine waited attentively to hear what he would say next, but then both flight attendants entered the cabin to make sure they were prepared for landing.

"That was nice, that's all," he said.

Elaine rubbed the skin of her neck, remembering how Zach's hand had caressed her there. "Oh." She cleared her throat. "So, can I ask where we're going?"

He smirked. "No, you may not, but I will say that first, I have some business to attend to. I would like for you to join me."

"Your business or our business?"

"My business."

"Then why—"

He raised a finger. "No questions."

Elaine sighed dejectedly. Going along for the ride was something she was never good at. It was strange that he wanted her to do a ride-along as he handled what was perhaps a business deal. She thought maybe he needed her legal advice. If so, then she would charge for her services, that was for sure.

"But I would like to know what's your favorite part of the city," he said.

"Huh?" That question came out of left field.

"Your favorite part of New York City."

Already feeling sour from being so powerless, Elaine curled her top lip. "I have no favorite part of that city."

"Everybody has a favorite part of the city."

"Not me."

"We'll have to change that."

Elaine sighed heavily. "You only have one day with me, and then you're going to give me back my shares."

Deep inside, she didn't believe a word of what she'd said. And from Zach's beaming expression, he hadn't believed her either.

ZACH SEEMED TO ALWAYS BE THE GENTLEMAN, opening doors for her, making sure he was on the right side of the walkway, not allowing her to pay for the latte she so desperately needed after they landed. As a matter of fact, he told her that part of their deal was for her to keep her cash and credit cards in her wallet. He was taking care of her for as long as they were together. That made Elaine feel jumpy.

They were leaving the Teterboro area on their way to Manhattan. Zach was driving them in the same kind of SUV he drove in LA. She wanted to make a little joke about it, but the uneasiness she felt was too stifling.

"Do you always drive yourself around New York?" she asked.

"Mostly, yes." He glanced at her with a grin that set her panties on fire.

"Most people of your stature who work in the city hire drivers."

He did it again—looked at her in his sexy way. "I know. But I get a rush from finding my way around traffic jams and shaking my fist while honking at cab drivers and shit. It makes me feel like a real New Yorker."

"I thought you were from LA."

"I grew up in Stamford, Connecticut, but we kept an apartment in the city since both my parents taught at Columbia U."

"But does that make you a real New Yorker?"

"I never said I was a real New Yorker, but I like to feel like one. Mix it up, you know?" He glanced at her with an exaggerated smile.

Elaine looked down at her lap, blushing. Whenever she came to the city, which was only for business, the people were more like wallpaper or amusement park puppets interacting in the fairyland they were built for. And she always hired a car to drive her around the city. Then when her business was over, she would go straight to the airport to get the hell out of Dodge.

"You do a lot of thinking," Zach said.

When she peered at him, he was already looking at her.

"I like that about you," he said.

She quickly turned away from him to gaze out the windshield as she waited for that faint feeling to pass.

The traffic did not disappoint. In the past, while sitting in the back seat and surrounded by tinted windows, she never felt compelled to focus on what was going on outside the car. Zach darted from one lane to the next and sometimes dashed down virtually empty streets. Elaine squeezed the door handle as she watched it all, forcing herself to remain quiet. She wanted to see what he meant by "mixing it up with the locals" when it came to driving.

But it was not just the drivers who were selective about which traffic laws to follow. Pedestrians would walk right in front of Zach's two tons of hot, speeding metal as though they didn't have a care in the world. Zach wouldn't slow down, either, but miraculously, he avoided a collision. Finally, they reached one of the thousands of skyscrapers. Zach parked in front of the building then told her stay put as he hopped out of the driver's seat and opened the door for her. Elaine didn't mind that. As soon as her feet hit the ground, her legs felt like jelly.

She put a hand on Zach's shoulder. "Okay, could you leave the crazy driving to the natives for the rest of the day? Could I at least ask you to do that?"

He snorted. "Done."

The valet parking attendant asked Zach for his ID, and he obliged.

"Thank you, Mr. Lord," the young guy said before stepping aside to let them pass.

Zach put his arm around Elaine's waist as they walked through the revolving glass doors and into the grand lobby. She was okay with having the extra support, because her legs were still recovering from that drive. He let go once they reached the front desk.

It felt so odd being there without really understanding her purpose. Still, she worked on not complaining, constantly reminding herself about the pot of thirty-nine shares at the end of the rainbow.

"Mr. Lord, welcome," the front desk attendant said, wearing a smile as wide and sparkly as the sun. It was clear not only that were they expecting Zach but also that his being there was important.

They were escorted to an elevator, and Zach put his arm around her again.

"I'm better, thank you," she said.

"I'm glad to hear it," he said but didn't move his arm.

Everything around them made the simple act of his arm being around her waist wrong. The gold-paneled walls of the elevators and the glossy white-stone floor made her want to put on her CEO cap. Instead, she felt like Zach's little lady, which seemed so out of line.

"Zach, could you please remove your arm?" she asked.

"Elaine?" He stepped in front of her and guided her against the gold wall. Now his hands were on both sides of her waist.

She gulped, surprised by what had just happened. "Huh?"

"I'm in control here. And remember our rules. You don't say anything. You don't ask questions. You trust me. I already promised I won't hurt you. I can't hurt you."

She wanted to fight and claw her way out of the situation, but she also wanted to succumb to his enchanting power. "Why can't you hurt me?" she asked breathlessly.

"Because I like you too much."

"Why?"

He slid his finger down the side of her face and the side of her neck. Elaine's heart felt as though it were going to explode. The elevator stopped, and the doors slid open.

"Hello, Mr. Lord," a woman said.

Elaine was breathing heavily, looking into his eyes. Suddenly, her lips wanted to float up to his. He had hypnotized her to the point that she no longer cared who was watching. Then he took a step back, turned around, and nodded at the woman, who was waiting for them.

"Hello," he said with an outstretched hand.

As the attractive woman shook Zach's hand, she glanced inquisitively at Elaine before her eyes landed back on his face.

"I'm Rita Masters, and we're happy you're here, Mr. Lord."

Zach put a hand on Elaine's waist, which sent tingles through her. "Rita, this is my colleague, Elaine Hester."

"Glad to meet you," Rita said as they shook hands.

He had taken his hand off her waist but made sure she stood by his side as Rita introduced them to Keith Noble and Ramsey Ling, the owners, who appeared to be in their midtwenties. Elaine was surprised by how small their company was. After the greetings were out of the way, Elaine and Zach were taken on a tour. She thought the gold-star treatment they had received in the lobby reflected the value of the operation. But nope. The offices were small, and the workers were cramped. First they were shown the accounting and finance and personnel offices. Keith explained that they had a lawyer offsite and gave Zach his name. They also paid to use the building's operations services.

"How much?" Zach asked.

Keith and Ramsey gave each other worried glances.

"Six thousand a month," Ramsey said. "But they do everything, give us coffee whenever we need it, greet our guests, give us access to executive elevators."

"By the way, how did you like your ride up?" Keith asked, grinning proudly.

Zach barely smiled. "It was nice."

The two guys looked at each other as if they'd just scored a point.

Next, Zach asked Keith and Ramsey to step away while he spoke to the workers. It was as though they expected his request, because without a look of surprise, they stepped out of the office. He insisted Elaine remain at his side as he walked through the space, talking to people and asking questions about what they did.

Elaine noticed he was very good at keeping them engaged in conversation long enough to make them let down their guard. Then they would reveal, however indirectly, how confused they were about what was going on around them half the time and how miraculous it was that everyone got paid at the end of the month. One thing they all believed in was the product, though. They knew what "their boys" created had been their bread and butter.

Zach made sure to shake every person's hand and thanked them for making him feel welcome before he rejoined Keith and Ramsey in the small reception area. Elaine could tell they were trying to read Zach's expression to learn whether he was impressed by their employees, but Zach kept an amazing poker face, which made him even more attractive. Then they went to what Keith called the brain center of their company, and he explained step-by-step how their new product was already revolutionizing the security of all technological products.

"It's been in the government sector for the last eighteen months," Keith said.

"And thirty-nine US-based companies have been granted permission to purchase the product from us, and they all love it," Ramsey said.

"We've just been given clearance to take it public, and we're ready to blow the top off the world," Keith said.

Elaine wanted to chuckle, but she didn't. Keith was hoping his enthusiasm would infect Zach, but it didn't. Once again, Elaine had to battle her desire to grab Zach and feverishly make out. His cool yet dominating manner was so alluring.

"Let's talk," Zach said.

The two owners beamed at each other before leading them to a conference room.

"Really?" Keith asked.

Zach nodded briskly. "Yes. But first, I'll need a moment to confer with my colleague, in private."

The two guys looked worried again but did as Zach asked. "Oh, sure," one of them said as he escorted them to another office, sounding a tad relieved.

Then Zach narrowed his eyes to search down the hallway on the opposite side of the reception area, away from everything else. "How about one of those rooms?"

Ramsey's eyes widened. "Um, those are our offices."

"Which is which?" Zach asked.

"Mine is on the right. Keith's is on the left."

Zach nodded firmly. "We'll take the left."

Elaine was lost about whatever Zach wanted to say to her. After all, it was her job to remain silent. She tried to think of some legal pointers she might want to give him, and she had a few. But once they were alone, the hungry look in Zach's eyes revealed exactly why he wanted time alone with her.

"So did you see out there?" he asked.

Elaine felt as confused as she looked. "What do you mean? What did I see?"

He stepped so close that she could feel the heat of his breath. "What did you see out there?"

Elaine felt choked up at first. Then she coughed to clear her throat. "An office."

"And who was in the office?"

"Employees."

"People, Elaine," he whispered, gently petting the side of her face down to her neck. "You're so fucking soft."

Her lips parted, but she had no idea how to respond to such a compliment.

"People can make or break your business, no matter how great your product is. You keep them happy on top of all the shit they have going on outside the walls of your business, and _you_ will succeed."

"Me?" she whispered.

"Yes, you."

Suddenly, they were kissing. Her head was floating. Then he lifted her off the ground, as if she were as light as a feather, and sat her on the desk. He pulled up her skirt, parted her knees, and yanked the crotch of her panties to the side. He dropped one knee down on the large black rug and then the other, never breaking eye contact. He tugged her lower half closer to his mouth.

Was he really going to perform oral sex on her? Here? Now? Then she felt his soft, warm mouth against her clit, and a tingling surprise swirled through her pussy. The erotic sensation made Elaine gasp and close her eyes to bear the next sensation, then the next, and more after that.

Zach moaned and groaned as though he was completely enjoying himself. Elaine could hardly endure the pleasure and stay quiet at the same time. She wanted to scream and call out to the Almighty. Then she tried to grab hold of something, but there was nothing she could grasp.

"Zach," she whimpered over and over again.

Her voice seemed to energize him, and he gave her hips no wiggle room. All Elaine could do was whimper and let her head roll back while allowing the deliciousness to fill her until she exploded in an orgasm, slapping a hand over her mouth to muffle her cries of passion.

Zach rose to his feet. Her legs were still spread as he glided his finger up and down her wetness. "May I enter you?" he asked.

Elaine's hazy gaze rolled around the room. She wanted nothing more than what he was asking for, but unplanned and unsafe sex was never her style. "Do you have a condom?" she asked.

Zach sank two fingers in and out of her. "No, but don't move an inch. And I mean it, not an inch." He raised his eyebrows in warning.

She nodded then watched as he started opening the first desk drawer.

"See, cocaine," he said.

Elaine stretched her neck, and to her shock, there was actually white powder in the desk. "Wow. Oh my goodness."

He closed the desk drawer and opened another. "This is Keith's office."

"How can you tell?" Elaine asked, because she hadn't been able to.

He pointed at the opposite side of the room. "That, on the wall."

She heard him open and close another drawer as she frowned at a framed portrait of a billion-dollar bill, which of course did not exist in real life. After more scrutiny, she noticed Keith's face in the center of the bill. Elaine snorted.

"Found them," Zach said, and she turned to see him take a condom out of a box.

"How did you know?" she asked.

Zach was standing between her legs again. He

unzipped his pants, and his rigid manhood sprang forward. "Because to do what I do, I have to know human behavior. The kid's making up for years of rejection. My guess is he does a hooker a day, at least." He winked.

Elaine's mouth fell open. With his tight pants and T-shirt that read "Born To Be Me" across the front, Keith looked nothing like a cocaine-snorting, hooker-banging loser.

Zach was so ready, Elaine could hardly believe she'd inspired such an erection. She remembered how Gary had to struggle to get hard and keep it up. After rolling on the condom, Zach set the wrapper on the desk, gripped her by her butt cheeks, and slowly but eagerly slid his firmness deep inside her.

Elaine's head fell back as she released a sigh of pleasure on impact. She wrapped her arms around his neck as he glided in and out of her. He mumbled indecipherably as though he was enjoying every stroke. His every thrust was pure pleasure. Then their gazes connected, and he stopped. Elaine felt something so very foreign as she stared deeper into his eyes. He shifted in and out of her even more indulgently. Their lips came close without kissing. His warm breaths pressed against hers.

Then he held her tightly against him as he shuddered and grunted.

ZACH HAD SHOWN HER THE WASTEBASKET WITH four used condoms already in it.

Elaine shook her head. "What the hell." She continued straightening her panties and skirt. "And what the hell are we doing?"

Zach seized her and tugged her against him. "I've been wanting to taste you ever since we were on the plane. I wasn't expecting you to say yes to the second part." He chuckled. "But I'm glad you did."

Elaine sighed wearily. "I've lost my mind. And did they hear us? I think they heard us. I know they did."

Her favorite smirk was plastered across his lips. "Doesn't matter. When I asked them to take me somewhere we could talk, they knew I was in. Everyone knows that if I leave, I'm out. I ask to see more, then we go to the next step."

Goodness, that turned her on. "You're still going to take the next step?"

"With you? I hope." He regarded her playfully.

She rolled her eyes, although it felt good to know that he wanted her after she'd given *it* away so easily. "I meant with this company. For goodness' sake, you found cocaine and condoms in Keith's desk."

"My team has the focus they lack." He came close and kissed her tenderly. "It's all about the product. We're going to make it brand-new. Then they're going to make more money than they could ever dream of, and we'll all live happily ever after." He started kissing and nibbling her neck.

Elaine dropped her head back, sighing. She almost succumbed to the sensual sensations, but she quickly came to her senses and nudged him back. "Once here is enough."

Zach raised his eyebrows. "It's sounds as though you're saying there's a twice somewhere on the horizon."

She rolled her eyes playfully, and they kissed some more. Yes, it was going to happen. She was going to let him. It was too late. She could no longer deny Zachary Lord the pleasure of taking her whenever and wherever he wanted.

CHAPTER 8

*D*uring the next phase of their visit, Zach expertly and in detail let Keith and Ramsey know how much money they had wasted. And he told them that as soon as the contracts were signed, their operation would move to his building, which was only down the street. They'd have the same amenities, less the prostitutes and drugs. "Do that on your time if you must," he said.

The guys seemed excited about the move. But from the amused look both guys had given Elaine, it was evident they knew what she and Zach had done in the office. Instead of being embarrassed, Elaine pretended it hadn't happened and made sure that showed on her face.

"I'm sorry. Are you Elaine Hester of AMTA?" Keith asked as they stood to leave.

"Yes," she said, realizing that they had scrambled to find out who she was after meeting her.

"My girlfriend's a screenwriter, and she's good, fucking fantastic actually. She had an agent, but..."

"He or she screwed her over?" she asked.

"Yep."

"What's her name?"

"Aliyah Rainey."

"Have her send her work to my office," Elaine said. After what she and Zach had done in the privacy of one of those offices, she owed Keith one —or maybe twenty.

Keith grinned. "I'll do that. I'll certainly do that."

THIS TIME, ELAINE AND ZACH RODE THE MAIN elevator down. It stopped on just about each floor, which normally irritated the hell out of Elaine but not today. Maybe it was because she was standing against Zach and could feel his chest rising and falling against her back. He was alive. And he was making her feel so very alive as well.

He held her hand once they entered the lobby, but Elaine stopped walking. "Do I have to?"

"Have to what?" He frowned, appearing genuinely confused.

"Hold hands?" They'd had sex not too long ago, and she was beginning to feel as though they were a couple. She had to be careful. Even though she had derived pleasure from Zach Lord, she would still destroy him if need be.

"Does it hurt to hold my hand?"

"No, it doesn't, but…"

He waited for her to finish. "Laney, come on. Everything doesn't always have to be so cerebral with you. Continue throwing caution to the wind. It's sexy as hell."

"Are you trying to weaken my defenses so that you can steal my company right out from under me?"

He wrapped his arms around her. "No. I am not. I don't want your company. I brought you here to help you. I want to show you something."

Zach let go of her and took his cell phone out of his pocket. Then he showed her pictures of a fancy space that looked like an office. She was sure it was taken at her company when she saw the 360-degree views.

"What's this?" she asked.

"Do you know Cesar Martinez?"

Elaine frowned contemplatively. "No, that name doesn't ring a bell."

"It should. He's your operations manager."

Zach explained how Lorna had offered him that office right before Elaine had fired her. And how Cesar had told of all the secrecy surrounding the building of the office. Zach suspected they were building it for someone who was supposed to take over the company if Archie hadn't died. Zach suspected that someone was still out there, waiting in the wings.

"When were you going to tell me about this?"

"I was going to tell you this morning during our meeting."

"Oh," she said, remembering they were set to meet at eight o'clock.

He put his phone back in his pocket and held her hand again. "Two things. If you choose to keep your company, then get to know your employees, all of them. And secondly, I don't want to talk any more business today. I want you to let me show you a good time. How about that?"

Elaine raised a finger. "Just one thing. Can I ask one question, please?" She smiled.

He smiled back. "How can I say no when you look at me that way?"

She dropped her face to chuckle bashfully then got serious. "When you say 'if I choose to keep my company,' what do you mean by that?"

He looked her deep in her eyes, and she was struck by that familiar feeling of him being able to see all of her doubts. Elaine looked down, breaking eye contact.

"How about we talk about it later?" he said.

"Okay," she whispered. She felt too raw to get into it now.

Soon they were back in Zach's SUV. His driving was slightly tamer, but he was talking business with someone on the phone through his AirPods, which were stuffed in his ears. Elaine rested her head against the seat. It hit her yet again that she and Zach had banged! Or was it banging? Even though what they had done was so spontaneous, she had never felt so close to a man. What did that mean? Perhaps she should view their involvement as a no-strings-attached fling. That way, when he eventually broke her heart, it wouldn't hurt so much.

"Hey, are you okay?" he asked.

She rolled her head in his direction to face him. "I am," she said with a satisfied smile. And to her surprise, she really was.

He studied her carefully then put his focus back on the road. "I have a few more loose ends to tie up, then I'm all yours."

Another call rang on the console. They both looked as the name Mike Falk lit up on the screen.

Zach quickly declined Mike's call and placed another one. Elaine went rigid. It was as though her brain had just gotten a sharp dose of reality. She stared out the window and distractedly watched as he made a turn down a busy street then zoomed down another. Elaine didn't know much about New York City neighborhoods, but she did know they were in Tribeca. They were speeding down a narrow alley until Zach stopped in front of a garage door. It opened, and he drove in, but he hadn't arrived at their destination yet. What he'd entered was merely a lift. Up they went, and when they stopped, his vehicle was parked in a pristine garage.

He said goodbye to Tobey Frey, the guy whose name was on the console, then looked at her as though he was hungry for more of what they had done earlier. "I want to invite you in, but we would never make it out if I did."

Elaine swallowed the lump in her throat. "That's okay," she croaked. She cleared her throat again. "Your place looks nice."

His flirtatious smile mirrored hers. "Thanks," he said.

"But you better be careful because you're wearing your bank account on your sleeve."

"Thanks for warning me."

They chuckled until their locked gazes smoldered.

Elaine cleared her throat, refusing to look away. "So what's next?"

His face leaned toward hers. "Let's get the hell out of here before I toss my plans to show you the city."

Elaine was close to admitting that she didn't want to see any more of New York City than she already had. She'd rather spend the rest of their day together in bed since she'd already elected to throw caution to the wind. She'd seen many facets of Zach that turned her on like never before. She craved more, and perhaps whatever awaited them beyond the bed would satiate that yearning.

"So how are we getting around town if you're parking our chariot?"

His eyes danced. "Walk some, cab some, and then see what happens next."

"Humph," she said, nodding. "No plan, huh?"

Zach chuckled. "Not used to proceeding without a plan, are you?"

"Nope."

They smiled at each other.

"Can I kiss you, Laney?"

The way he looked at her took her breath—and words —away, so she nodded.

Their lips melted, then their tongues curled. Elaine's body burned with longing, and the longer they kissed, the more she let go. Her hands played through his hair and clawed at his strong shoulders and back.

Zach ripped his mouth off hers. "Let's get the hell out of here before it's too late."

ZACH HAILED A CAB BECAUSE ELAINE POINTED OUT that her shoes weren't made for walking, and frankly, even though it was a nice seventy degrees out, neither was the cap-sleeved, low-cut beige blouse of her Donna Karan skirt suit. Zach gave the cab driver the address of where they were going and told Elaine they were heading uptown. On the way over, he made a phone call to a friend and asked him or her to reserve a table for him later that evening. His tone had changed while he was talking to the person on the other line. He sounded hip and not at all like the billionaire CEO and owner of an investment firm.

Ever since the moment Zach had driven her to the airport in LA, Elaine had slowly stopped feeling like the owner of one of the largest talent agencies in the world. That definitely had something to do with her present company. She wasn't sure whether that was good or bad.

The cab stopped in front of Hamilton Goldsmith, and her mouth dropped. Elaine didn't mind shopping at such an expensive department store, but she would've rather personally paid for whatever she was going to buy.

"Laney, remember," he said, apparently reading her expression, "it's on me."

She faked a smile and hated that she couldn't negotiate with him, because he had convinced her to leave her purse locked in his car. She didn't even bring her ID, since Zach had said she wouldn't need it because she was with him.

"Let's try to get in and out in twenty minutes. Make it casual, comfortable. Pick two outfits," he said as though he were the coach calling the plays.

His directives made her cringe. First of all, she'd never shopped for clothing in less than two hours. "Twenty minutes? Impossible."

He smirked. "You can do it, Laney."

She rolled her eyes then her shoulders and sighed heavily. "Okay, I'll give it the old college try."

"Atta sexy-ass woman," he said.

And for that, she crashed her mouth against his and kissed him deeply. Although she started it, Zach was determined to finish. He lifted her onto his lap, kissed harder, and didn't stop until the cab driver reminded them that they were on the meter.

Zach took a hundred-dollar bill out of his wallet and handed it to the driver. "Come back in twenty-five minutes."

The taxi driver nodded.

"Twenty-five? I thought you said twenty," Elaine said.

"I decided to give you an extra five minutes." He winked then told her to stay put as he got out of the taxi and opened the door for her.

ONCE INSIDE, THEY RODE UP TO THE FIFTH FLOOR. Before heading to the men's section, Zach instructed her to let the salespeople know that she was there with him. It nearly killed Elaine to say, "Okay," but she did. A man buying her clothes? Up until that very moment, she truly hadn't believed it was going to happen. She was capable of purchasing her own attire. But of course, Zach knew that.

"Relax, Laney," she whispered. There was no use in making a mountain out of a molehill.

Elaine browsed through the neatly hung and folded clothes. She only wore casual attire when she was working in her garden, lounging around the house, or exercising. She was less than five minutes in and totally flustered. Thank goodness a saleswoman asked if she needed help. It was at that very moment that Elaine decided to imitate her sister's style. No one did barely-trying-but-still-sexy chic like Sonja.

"Yes," Elaine told the saleswoman. "I need two pairs of those jeans with the narrow legs. One pair with rips, you know, and the other pair black." Then she remembered something else about Sonja's everyday attire. "And make them faded, a little or a lot."

The saleswoman looked Elaine up and down. "Size four?"

"That's right," Elaine said with a smile.

"Then I'll be back with some options you might like." The woman started to walk away.

"Oh, and I need T-shirts, two of them. They have to be slightly fitted and also vintage looking. And I'll need a black leather moto jacket."

"You got it. Anything else?"

Elaine checked her watch. "Two things. I need to be out of here in thirteen minutes. I'm here with Zach Lord, and oops, make that three things…"

The woman smiled as though she weren't bothered at all by Elaine's franticness.

"I need canvas tennis shoes, comfortable, in a size—"

"Eight?"

"Yes!" Elaine said.

SHE HAD WON HER RACE AGAINST THE CLOCK. SHE even had time to put on one outfit while they neatly boxed the suit she'd been wearing. They said they would deliver it and the second outfit Zach had bought for her to his place. Of course, she didn't choose any of the garments that were "Sonja-like." After putting on a pair of ripped jeans, she decided to let Sonja be Sonja. But Lydia, the saleswoman, was an expert and helped her find a black stretchy spaghetti-strap dress and a pair of skinny red pants with a white V-neck T-shirt.

Elaine thanked Lydia profusely for using her superpowers as a saleswoman and stylist to figure out what she'd really wanted.

"I wish I could take credit for the black dress. Zachary Lord told me you would love it. So it was all him."

The funny thing was, that was the outfit Elaine had chosen to wear for the rest of the day.

When Zach saw her, he stared at her as though he was trapped in a daze. Lydia had even suggested she set her wild and curly locks free from the tight bun, which she rarely did. But she released her strands because she wanted Zach to have the reaction he was currently displaying.

Finally, he walked slowly and stood close to her and lowered his mouth to her ear. "It's taking all the willpower in the world to stop me from..." He sucked air.

Elaine closed her eyes to allow the dizzy feeling to pass. Zach was getting her all hot and bothered again.

"You look good too," she whispered and conjured an image of him in a fashionable black T-shirt and black chinos that fit his thighs and butt while perfectly emphasizing his height. What a stunningly gorgeous man. It was still hard to believe he didn't have a harem of women trailing him, waiting for their chance to be kissed and caressed by the sexy prince. It felt so good to be in his arms. He ran his lips up and down her neck; that felt divine.

He took her by the hand in a way that he'd been doing often, and they walked to the elevator and out of the department store, and that was when the fun began.

CHAPTER 9

*T*he alluring violet sky added to the excitement, and as promised, the cab was waiting for them out front. Zach opened the door and let her slide in first. He told the cab driver to head downtown and told him which street to travel.

"I'll let you know when we're ready to get out," Zach said to the driver.

The sidewalks of New York were similar to the 405 freeway in LA, constantly congested by traffic. But they were moving slowly enough for Elaine to get a good view of all the landmarks Zach pointed out. He wasn't showing her the touristy stuff, though, which she was grateful for, because she had taken that tour two times too many. Instead, he pointed out the cathedral where his parents were married and the movie theater where he had his first make-out session as a teenager. He directed her attention to a street corner where a guy named Pepper usually stood to recite the entire works of Shakespeare.

"But you can only catch him on Mondays, Wednesdays, and Thursdays."

"Why's that?" Elaine asked, nestled up against his chest, in love with being that close to him.

"He said the other days of the week were holy days."

"Holy?"

"Wholly reserved for vodka."

Elaine snorted cynically. "Now that's a way to kill your liver."

"We all get to choose how we live and die. At least we should," he said.

She mulled over his words. Had she ever subscribed to such a notion? Nope. Coming from Zach, it sounded like a tenet for life. If not a long life, then certainly a happy one. Oh, what a relief it would be to stop worrying about decisions made by her sister, cousins, employees, and just about everyone else in the world.

Zach turned her attention to spots where they

had the best hot dogs, bagels, pizza, pastries and coffee, jazz, alternative music, and big band hip-hop. She didn't miss any of what he pointed out because they were still inching along. Even though she was so hungry she could eat a horse, she hadn't ever experienced a slow ride up the avenue, and apparently neither had the cab driver. The longer they sat, the higher the toll.

Finally, Zach tapped the side of the front passenger seat and told the driver they were getting out, even if they were in the middle of a traffic jam. The taxi driver insisted he pull over to the curb first.

Zach took a wad of bills out of his wallet. "Do you want a tip or not?"

The driver took a glance at the cash and nodded briskly. Zach counted off a number of twenties and handed them to him. Elaine didn't attempt to count the cash. He had already spent way too much money on her. There was no need to keep tallying up the amount.

Zach said they were in Chelsea. Elaine couldn't tell when they had entered the neighborhood, but frankly, she didn't need to know. She was finally adhering to the program that Zach wanted for her that day, which was not to be thinking too hard about unnecessary things. She was with him. He would make sure she eventually arrived home safely. At least that was how she was feeling at the moment. The smell of food, however, was making her stomach cranky.

"Zach, I have to eat soon," she whined, which didn't sound like her at all.

Before she could say it again in a more adult tone, he swept her off her feet, and now he was cradling her.

She looked around to see who was watching them. "Why did you do that?" No one was paying them the slightest attention.

He kissed her lips. "I'm going to carry you the rest of way."

"No," she said, trying to wiggle out of his arms. "I'm fine. I can walk."

"Laney?" he said suddenly.

"What?"

"Let me carry you. I like it when you're in my arms."

Elaine could feel her eyes frown intensely as he continued walking with her in his arms, even though she felt uncomfortable. She had two feet. Yeah, she was starving and for more than just food, but Elaine was a strong woman. All of her self-esteem had been built upon that foundation. But when he made a quick turn and started down a narrow, dimly lit and stinky alley, she became very happy that her shoes were not planted on the filthy ground. She wouldn't know what to do if she had stepped on a dead rat or something.

Zach stopped in front of a red metal door.

"Knock three times fast and then twice slowly," he said.

Elaine jerked her head. "Really?"

He smirked and flexed an eyebrow twice. The way he looked while doing that made her head feel as if she'd been hit by a dose of silly gas. It was too much. He was too much. There was no way Zach's treatment of her was genuine.

"Are you a serial killer in real life or something? Right now you're all charming and perfect, but later you're going to lower the hatchet over my neck, figuratively or literally?"

He looked disturbed by her question. "Why did you ask that?"

"The way you're treating me. It's like you're charming me. I'm meat you're tenderizing. You're getting me ready so you can do something hurtful in the future."

He closed his eyes as though he had to absorb her words. "Elaine, I said I would never hurt you, and I mean that. You want your shares, you have them. Come tomorrow morning, I'll have my accountant issue them to you, and you'll receive the paperwork on your desk by Monday afternoon at the latest. As far as your heart's concerned, I think I've been pretty clear about what I want."

She shook her head adamantly. "No, you haven't."

"Yes, I have," he said staunchly. "Do you think I'd do all this for just any woman?"

Elaine scrunched one side of her face. "I kind of do."

"Well, I don't. And you're going to have to trust me, or any other man that you can't control. But shit, Elaine, I hope it's me you learn to trust, 'cause I want to see how far we can take this."

How far they could take this? She wanted to deconstruct all he'd said, but all lines of reasoning would've led to two thought-provoking questions. Did she deserve a man like Zach Lord? And why in the hell did she believe she didn't?

"Elaine?" he asked.

"Yes." She had been distracted by her thoughts.

"If we stand out here any longer, then I may end up having to fight a serial killer to keep you safe."

"Oh, right," she said. "It's three fast knocks, two slower ones."

He kissed her tenderly, just enough to take her breath away.

"Yes," he whispered.

She sighed and then did it.

Knock-knock-knock. Knock, knock.

FROM THE MOMENT THE DOOR OPENED, THINGS went fast. Zach knew the doorman, the waitstaff, and a majority of the patrons. She asked if he owned the place, and he said no. It was just one of his favorite hidden gems the city had to offer, and tonight he wanted to share it with her.

It wasn't a five-star restaurant on the Upper East Side, which was where she usually dined whenever she came to town on business. Every single first date she'd ever had was with some guy who tried to impress her with an expensive meal while leaving a shabby tip. Or even worse, some nouveau riche douchebag—usually a real estate developer—would take her to some nightclub where bottle service cost an arm, a leg, and both kidneys and the music was so loud it took at least two days to recover. Looking at how casual everyone appeared and how the restaurant wasn't crowded with hip yuppies out to be seen, Elaine was starting to trust the affection Zach had been bestowing upon her.

They were seated at a round table painted black. The chairs were upholstered with black faux fur. The walls were covered in metallic black wallpaper, and the floor was black and white checkered. After the waitress looked at them, she didn't hand them a menu, but still, Zach ordered. "Both."

"What's both?" she asked.

"Spaghetti and meatballs and chicken cacciatore. That's all they serve here. But you'll like it, I promise."

"Like it?" She narrowed an eye coyly.

"Okay, love it."

Elaine smiled. "That's better."

With only two dishes served, the food arrived fast. She was very surprised at how it was plated, as though it were being served in a Michelin star restaurant. Just before digging in, they were joined by two of Zach's friends. One was named Sparrow, perhaps because of how his forehead and nose were attached in one long straight line while his chin was short. But those were the only parts of him that resembled a bird. He was tall and thin. The other guy, Ernie, was short and stout and had an extremely receding hairline. The hair hanging from the sides of his head was really long and curly. He could've definitely benefited from a good and wise barber who would advise him to shave every strand of hair left on his head. Zach and his friends were picking up where their previous conversation— which had occurred a while ago—left off. Sparrow was saying that Zach had been right about the mating rituals of penguins. He'd had to do research, but what Zach had said was true, and the fact that male penguins returned to Iceland year after year to fuck the same female penguin changed Sparrow's belief system forever.

Ernie raised a finger and objected. "Unless the female is eaten by a seal. Then he fucks a different female."

"Or she's eaten by a walrus," Zach added and winked at Elaine.

"Oh, yes, right, right," Sparrow said, as though Zach had just made an exceptionally astute point.

Elaine couldn't believe she was smiling at their stupid conversation. Had she ever allowed herself to participate in such triviality? Robin, Theresa, and Sonja would every now and then engage in point-less discussions, but Elaine had never joined them.

At times, she found herself laughing at the men's conversation, especially when Sparrow said that as soon as he learned the fate of a male penguin, he'd called the New York Aquarium and asked if there was a male penguin he could buy.

"One that had lost his seasonal fuck buddy."

"Oh, smart… smart," Ernie said, nodding.

Not smart, Elaine thought, and although she wanted to say it out loud, she bit her tongue.

"So the girl hangs up on me," Sparrow said. "I call back, four times. The final time, this gal says to me, 'Sir, thank you for caring about penguins. I'm positive they appreciate your advocacy, but if you want to ensure the survival of just one more male penguin, then stop calling this fucking zoo asking for one.'"

Elaine erupted with laughter so infectious that Zach laughed with her. Sparrow and Ernie looked perplexed by what she had found so funny.

"I'm sorry, so sorry," Elaine said, forcing herself to quiet down. "Please continue. What happened next?"

Sparrow's brows wrinkled and then relaxed. "I didn't agree with her. Hell, I never took care of a kid, but I could take care of a fucking penguin. That's what I told her."

"And what did she say?" Elaine asked, staring at his mouth.

"She said I would have to move to Antarctica or Alaska if I wanted a penguin. Do you think I want to move to Alaska? Fuck no."

Ernie sat back in his chair, shaking his head. "Nah, I wouldn't do that either."

It was hard to believe they were sincere about such craziness. But at least the conversation had gone in a different direction. They were talking about how cold it got in New York and were recalling the worst winters to date.

The food was fantastic, and Elaine felt more relaxed than she ever had. She loved the fact that she could easily let them have their conversation without her judgment or need to convince them to think the way she did.

"Has anyone ever told you you look like, um…" Sparrow said then snapped his fingers.

Elaine noted that while he kept saying, "Um," that didn't annoy her either.

"Ah, bloody hell," Ernie said in an English accent that just came out of nowhere. "Audrey Hepburn."

Sparrow shook his finger. "That's who she resembles. But you're more beautiful."

It wasn't the first time Elaine had been compared to the actress of old, but she blushed, anyway.

"But isn't that interesting about penguins?" Sparrow asked.

Elaine was shocked. She thought he was done with the penguins already.

Zach drummed on the tabletop. "I would love to hear more about the fucking penguins, but Audrey Elaine and I have to blow this joint."

He stood, and so did Elaine.

Sparrow snapped his fingers. "Is that her name, Audrey Elaine? Because she resembles Audrey Hepburn."

"But prettier," Ernie said.

Zach held Elaine's hand. "I think we've established that already. Another day, another debate, fellas."

Out of nowhere, a woman with long raven hair, milky olive skin, and jeans so tight it was a miracle she was able to get in them appeared on the other side of Zach's shoulder.

"Hello, handsome," she purred with a Spanish accent. "I did not know you were here tonight. Let's have a drink."

At first Zach looked at her as though he didn't

recognize her. "Graciela?" he asked and wrapped one arm around Elaine's waist.

"Zach," she said with attitude.

"Right, Graciela. We're about to leave." His tone was formal.

Graciela didn't even sneak a peek at Elaine. Instead, she kept her flirtatious gaze on Zach's face. "Then stay. I know you remember how much I'm worth it."

Zach glanced nervously at Elaine. He was probably only pretending not to remember Graciela. She was just the sort of woman that Elaine suspected he gravitated toward, so very different from herself.

Elaine desperately wanted to escape the scene and leave Zach with the sort of woman she felt he really wanted. But she was trapped. Her purse was in Zach's SUV, parked in his private garage. No one in her family knew where she was. She could've called Sonja, who should be back in town by now. But would Sonja help her? That would be a first.

Finally, the woman glanced at Elaine. "Oh, but I can wait my turn. You said you were going to show me how to…" She stood on the tip of her toes, which were being supported by very high and skinny heels, then whispered something in his ear.

That was it. "I'm leaving," Elaine said in his other ear and tried to rip herself out of his hold.

"Graciela, Sparrow, Ernie, good night," Zach said.

As they walked to the exit, Elaine felt all her hopes about being with Zach come crashing down. She was hurt. They passed a waitress, who said goodbye to Zach with her flirty eyes. Perhaps she was another woman he had been involved with.

"Take me home," Elaine said as soon as the stepped into the alley. The next thing she knew, she was against the wall, and Zach's tongue was in her mouth.

She ripped her head to the side to break lip contact.

"Fuck, Elaine, I can hardly remember Graciela."

She tried to push him off of her, but he was too strong. "Don't lie to me."

"I wouldn't lie to you. I would tell you the fucking truth."

Her glare latched onto the light and the busy sidewalk at the end of the alley. "Have you ever slept with her?"

Zach sighed. "That's not fair."

"Have you?"

"A long time ago."

She tried to wiggle her way out of his grasp. "Let me go."

"First hear me out, and then I'll do whatever you ask."

"And still give me my shares."

"You already have my word on that."

Finally, she turned to look into his eyes. Elaine took a deep breath. Was she overreacting?

"You're not the first woman in my life, but you are the first complete package."

"I'm not in your life. We just met yesterday."

"Exactly. I've been trying to prove myself to you since the moment I saw you." Finally, he let go of her. "Am I fucking crazy? Am I wasting my time?"

Elaine closed her eyes to think. She was never one to play hard to get. Either she wanted to start something with a guy, or she didn't. What Zach was bringing to her life was new and grand. Did she really want it to end? So she sighed gravely and muttered, "No."

"No?" He sounded encouraged.

She dropped her head. "No. You're not wasting your time. I like you, Zach. I like you a lot."

"I like you too. And I promise you, I haven't

seen Graciela in ages. She's crazy as hell, though. Way crazier than you are."

She lifted her head. He was grinning.

Elaine snickered. "I'm crazy?"

"In a good way."

They stared into each other's eyes. Zach slid the back of his hand down the side of her forehead, cheek, and neck.

"Laney, all I want to do is be with you, a lot. In many ways. That's it. Is that okay?"

Elaine was too choked up to say anything. Was Zach Lord a real person? Of course he was. But she still wondered if she deserved such a man. Was she nice enough? Was she lovable enough? Then she heard something squeak near her feet. She looked down and saw a rodent scampering up the alley.

"Yes, it's okay," she said in a rush. "Now we can go. And could you carry me to the sidewalk?" Since she hadn't walked into the alley, she preferred not to walk out of it, either.

Zach grinned from ear to ear then swept her off her feet and into his arms. He carted her out to the sidewalk and didn't put her down, even while hailing a cab. After sliding into the back seat, he told the driver they were heading to East Harlem and gave the driver the address.

"What are we doing in Harlem?" Elaine asked. She'd never been to that part of the city but had always wanted to go.

"It's a surprise."

Their faces stayed close as they kissed and stared into each other's eyes. Her heart had never gone through so many variations of excitement. On the streets, there was less traffic, and it was going on eleven o'clock. Normally Elaine would be in bed by that time, exhausted, but her mind would be thinking about all of her worries, making it difficult to fall asleep. But tonight she was wide awake and feeling as though she were having an out-of-body experience, watching someone else have a life she could never have dreamt of.

"Lady," the cab driver said in an Indian accent.

Elaine saw his eyes watching her through the rearview mirror.

"Sir?"

"Where are you from?"

Her eyes expanded, shocked by his intrusion into her personal life.

"Tell him, Laney," Zach whispered in her ear. "You look interesting."

"Um, I'm from Los Angeles," Elaine said.

"Hollywood is there?" he asked.

She shifted uncomfortably in her seat. "Um, yeah. Actually, it's where I grew up."

When he asked if she knew certain movie stars, she said yes and was able to tell him all about his favorites, at least the stuff that wouldn't end their careers.

———

THE DRIVER DROPPED THEM OFF IN FRONT OF A redbrick building, but half the span of the street-level floor was one space with tinted glass windows. As soon as they got out of the cab, she could hear jazz.

"Music?" Elaine asked.

He kissed her. "Let's dance."

She squeezed both his hands tightly. "But I can't dance."

"Babe, you're sexy. Just be sexy, for me." His eyes smoldered.

Her breath caught as he guided her past a line and to the front entrance.

"Zachary Lord," the doorman sang once he saw them.

They slapped hands.

The guy asked Zach a question, but his New

York accent was so thick that Elaine couldn't make out what he said.

"Yes, thank you," Zach replied.

They walked past the cashier without paying.

"Someone who used to work for me owns the place," he said as he placed his hands on her hips, leading her past crowded tables on their way to the dance floor. Elaine felt as though she were in a sexy, hazy, and euphoric dream as she watched heads bop and shoulders swing under the hazy red-and-blue lights.

Her feet finally hit the parquet, and Zach twirled her with ease then guided her body against his. Grinding her with his hard-on. The fact that he was so excited already made her thighs quiver. So she let the sensual energy flowing between them guide her moves. She grinded him back, twisting her hips slowly, maintaining eye contact as every bit of her soul wanted Zach to consume her.

The songs changed, but even when they were fast, Zach held her against him and indulged in all his favorite parts of her body.

At some point a guy tapped him on the shoulder and asked to cut in, but Zach said something to him, and he went away.

"What did you say?" she asked.

"I told him tonight, you're all mine. The next time we come, you'll owe him a dance, though."

Elaine chuckled. "Are you keeping dance cards?"

He twirled, dipped her, and then kissed her deeply.

AT TIMES THEY WOULD STOP AND CLAP WHILE THEY watched a live band that had taken the stage. Zach couldn't keep his hands off her ass, waist, and tits. Elaine was having the time of her life. Sonja, Terry, and Robin would never believe she was doing what she was doing. And she liked it! No. She loved it.

They never sat down, even just to wet their whistles. Once he was done dancing with her, Zach announced he had one more place to take her. They'd get drinks there. When they walked out of the nightclub, a hired car was waiting for them.

"You do have one," she teased.

He smirked and winked at her. Damn, she loved it when he did that.

"I like to diversify."

She chuckled.

Once they slid into the back seat, she knew exactly why Zach had called his hired car. A tinted window separated the front from the back. Her legs were spread. His face was between them. And before they reached their destination, she had climaxed three times.

———

THE CAR STOPPED IN FRONT OF WHAT LOOKED LIKE an abandoned industrial building. Zach said they were in Brooklyn. After experiencing what she had during the car ride, Elaine's legs were so wobbly she could hardly stand.

Once they walked inside, they had to climb a set of clunky steps before making it to a room filled wall-to-wall with pool tables. Some 1990s Top 40 music played in the background. The atmosphere was vaporous but not from cigarettes, cigars, or any other smoked products.

Zach said the fog was purified air. "You're going to feel good for a long time after we leave." The sexy way he flexed his eyebrows made her love the sound of that.

Also, it was one o'clock in the morning, and a lot of people were still there. None of them looked as if they were anywhere near ready to call it a night, either.

They were greeted by a college-aged girl wearing a short black skirt and a tank top with embroidered pool balls on it. She escorted them to the table Zach had already reserved.

"Can I get you something to drink?" she asked, flapping her eyelashes flirtatiously at Zach.

"Scotch on the rocks for me," he said, then he examined Elaine with one eye narrowed. "A red wine. No. Pear brandy in a snifter."

The almost tipsy mood her endorphins had put her in had made her grin agreeably and not insist on the red wine. She'd never had pear brandy before but certainly was up for trying it.

"Trust me, you're going to like it," he said.

The waitress watched as they simpered at each other. After they'd had sex in the car on the way over, the dancing, and what he did to her in Keith's office, she was horny as hell.

Then Zach made himself break contact with her to grab two pool sticks. "Do you know how to play?" he asked, handing her one.

"You'll just have to try me and see."

The smirk.

Her head spun.

He racked them up, and she broke. It was an excellent shot.

Zach walked around the table and tugged her against him. "If you're hustling me, then you better watch out because it's turning me on."

They kissed so intensely that she dropped the pool stick. It could've been the pure air or all the orgasms she'd had in one day, but Elaine was ready to blow that joint and get between the sheets with Zach.

"Laney?"

Elaine tensed as her lips froze mid-kiss. She recognized the voice and quickly turned to look behind her. "Sonja?"

"It *is* you. What the hell are you doing in New York?" Sonja's eyes kept shifting from Zach's face to Elaine's.

"I'm in town on business. What are you doing here? In the pool place, I mean. Playing pool?"

Sonja couldn't pull her curious gaze from Zach. "Oh," she finally said. "You're the guy who came to the table while they were having dinner last night."

Elaine groaned as she shook her head, then she looked at Zach. "That's how fast news travels in my family."

Jay walked up behind Sonja and put his arms around her. "It is you!" he sang. "You look"—he zigzagged the finger he pointed at her—"different."

She was still too shocked, and slightly embarrassed about how she looked and felt, to say something.

"Hi, I'm Zach." He shook Sonja and Jay's hands.

Sonja's eyes danced with amusement. "So you're the inspiration behind this change in my sister?"

"Stop, Son," Elaine snapped.

"I hope so," Zach said and winked at Elaine.

That one wink, for a moment, made her feel as if they were the only two people in the room.

"Oh," Sonja said. "I see… Okay." She sounded totally discombobulated.

"Hey, man, I saw Laney's break. Don't let yourself get hustled by the Hester girls," Jay said.

Zach laughed. "I'm okay with it."

"Actually, I am too."

"So you're the actor, Jay West."

"In the flesh."

Elaine and Sonja couldn't stop staring at each other as Zach ran down a short list of Jay's movies that he liked.

"So you're married now," Elaine said, grinning tightly at Sonja. Truth be told, she wasn't so sour about it anymore.

"Yes, Laney," Sonja said. "And you were right. Gran wants to see us tie the knot, so we were thinking of having a real ceremony in your backyard in a few weeks. How's that sound?"

Elaine looked from Jay to Zach and then back at Sonja. "Um…"

"Wait. Did you say 'Um'?" Sonja asked.

"Yeah, well, I don't think I'm ready for the headache of hosting a full-on wedding."

"I'm not asking you to host it. I'm going to pay someone to do it. I know you're busy, Laney. But busy or not, all I want you to do is sit back and enjoy the day."

Elaine closed her eyes to think about it. Then their drinks arrived.

It wasn't until after she tasted the peach brandy, which was divine, that the answer her heart was trying to convey rose to the surface. "Okay, I'll just be a guest, and that's all."

Sonja jerked her head back. "No changing the flowers, yelling at the caterers, or hiring extra ushers?" She raised a finger. "Oh, or reordering the cake to your specifications?"

"I'll do only what you ask, maybe."

Sonja grabbed Elaine by the shoulders and shook her lightly. "Okay, but where's my sister, and what have you done with her? Although I like this you slightly better, but I mean, are you, like, dying or something and it's sparking this rapid change in you?"

Elaine rolled her eyes hard. "Stop exaggerating, Son. And rack them up. I'm ready to kick your ass for getting married before I did."

Sonja laughed as they hugged.

"Now there's the bitter bitch I love to the moon and back!" She kissed Elaine on the cheek then whispered in her ear, "And thank God none of those losers stuck, because oh my God, Laney, this Zach guy. Well done."

She snickered. It wasn't as though Zach didn't hear her. Sonja was the worst whisperer in the world.

Sonja and Elaine played a game of pool against each other. Zach was her cheerleader, and Jay was Sonja's. It got super competitive, and Elaine was one shot away from winning bragging rights, but her finger slipped off the stick when three other people came over to join them. One of them someone she'd thought Zach would never meet.

CHAPTER 10

"Charlie Lord," the guy said as they shook hands.

Zach frowned at Elaine. If it weren't for the fact that he had coaxed her into coming to New York and her cell phone had been locked in his Range Rover all day, he would've suspected her of setting him up. She hadn't told him that she knew Charlie Lord.

"Zach Lord," he said and waited for Charlie's reaction.

"Ah, we share the same last name," Charlie said and chuckled. "That's cool."

Zach didn't know whether to be relieved or disappointed that his second cousin didn't know him from Adam. He had a beautiful woman with him, whom Sonja had just introduced to Elaine and Zach. Her name was Angelina, but she said to call her Angel.

"Are you two related?" Angel asked, looking from Charlie to Zach. "You look related."

"I wouldn't know," Charlie said. "But Jack would."

Zach knew the answer, and if he didn't say something now, he would be dishonest. "Actually, we're cousins," Zach said. "We've met before, about four years ago."

"Ah, I must've been inebriated," Charlie said.

Zack snorted. "You were drunk, in a bar. Probably high too."

"Sounds about right."

"My grandfather is Bentley Lord, and yours is Charles—"

"The first," Charlie said and threw his arms up. "Then we're family."

They hugged loosely.

"Indeed," Zach said.

Sonja took advantage of Elaine's error and won their first game, but they decided to go the best out of three. Zach couldn't take his eyes off Elaine in that black dress. Ever since he first saw her in it, he'd struggled with the intense desire to rip it off her and make love to her until he ran out of steam. Shit, she tasted so good. He was amazed by his ability to keep up with Charlie, who was a talker, and still lust after the woman he couldn't wait to devour.

His distant cousin had just told him they were in town to see Jacques Blanchard's "One Night Only" concert.

"Get the fuck out of here," Zach exclaimed. It was the first time he could actually rip his eyes off Elaine. "I've been trying to get tickets for that damn concert for months. And I can buy my way into any fucking concert I want."

"You want in? We'll get you in. The both of you." He pointed his head at Angel, his wife. "See that beautiful specimen over there?"

Angel was having a conversation with the guy who had introduced himself as Dexter Frampton, who Zach thought was attracted to Elaine until Dexter asked her how Robin was doing these days.

"Robin's Robin," Elaine had said.

"That's the same answer I always get from Sonja," he said.

"Because it's true," Elaine and Sonja said at the same time.

Zach smiled as he remembered that moment and focused on Angel. "Yeah, I see her," he said, answering Charlie's question.

"She's Jacques's daughter," he said proudly, regarding her in the same manner he'd been watching Elaine.

Zach stood up straight, trying to contain his excitement. "Get the hell out of here."

Charlie smiled broadly as he nodded.

"Yes, we want to go," Zach affirmed.

"The concert's tomorrow night. We're all going on one of those party buses." He shrugged. "My wife's idea. But Jack, my brother, and his wife, Daisy, who's my wife's sister, will be with us."

Zach raised a hand. "Wait. Your brother is married to her sister?"

Charlie snorted. "It's a long story but a good one."

Zach chuckled. "I bet it is."

"I would ask how in the hell we never met while I was sober, but if your grandfather is or was anything like mine, then there's the answer."

"An ornery, angry, and hateful old bastard?" Zach asked.

"In the flesh."

They went on to talk about their fathers, and Charlie's story was shorter than Zach's. At least Zach's dad, Langston, was still alive and a good guy, information that he shared with his cousin.

"He lives in Connecticut, huh?" Charlie asked.

"Yeah, and he still teaches at Columbia."

"I'd like to meet him someday. He sounds like a unicorn as far as our forefathers are concerned."

Zach snorted. He could appreciate Charlie's cynicism regarding the men who came before them. Then Zach recalled a memory that had been lost for many years.

"My grandfather slapped me once," he confessed out of the blue. "I forgot what for. I guess for being a kid. That was the last I ever saw him. My father cut him off after that."

"Wow," Charlie said, as if Zach's revelation had taken his breath away. "Damn, I have to meet this guy, Langston. I need to see some fucking redeeming qualities," Charlie said, shaking his head. He went on to tell Zach how Jacques Blanchard had become something of a surrogate father to him from the first day they had met.

Over at the pool table, Elaine won the second round. She looked so free and cute, jumping up and down celebrating. Zach would've rather she bowed out of the third round, but she was having a lot of fun, and watching her was the greatest show on earth. But he had been waiting all day to lay her in his bed and make love to her. He needed her body, and he needed her soon. Yet he didn't want to stop talking to Charlie Lord.

Zach learned Charlie and Angel had bought a place in the city because they were in town often. Angel, her sister, and his cousin Maggie wanted their children to be close. Also, Angel was a dancer and Charlie a musician, so they often worked on Broadway shows, either together or apart. It was cool to learn he and his cousin frequented many of the same spots, which included the two he and Elaine had visited that night.

When Sonja won the third game, Elaine congratulated her with a hug.

Zach stood to retrieve his wallet out of his pocket and gave Charlie his card. "Listen, it was an honor to talk to you."

Charlie rose to his feet. "Same here. And I don't carry business cards when I'm out like this, so I can't return the gesture, but what's your address? We'll swing by around seven tomorrow to pick you up."

Zach gave him the address.

Charlie slammed his hands on his waist and hung his head. "What the hell, really?" He raised his head. "Our apartment is in that building."

Zach could hardly believe what Charlie had just revealed. It all seemed too cosmic. Butch had died, he'd met Elaine, and her sister associated with his distant cousins.

ON THE WAY BACK TO HIS PLACE, ELAINE HAD fallen asleep on his chest. She'd had three pear brandies, and for a lightweight, that meant lights out. Zach wasn't all that disappointed. He was exhausted, too, mentally more than emotionally.

Zach had always had a zest for life and happiness. Sure, he made a lot of money for others and himself, but it all came from the heart. He loved what he did. Charlie loved what he did too. When Zach's grandfather Bentley died, he left millions to Zach's father, Langston. But there were stipulations to the inheritance. First, Langston would've had to divorce Zach's mother simply because she was not a WASP. Secondly, he would've had to stop "playing with fossils and old clay," as his grandfather would have said, and run their family's portion of the Lords' steel business.

Langston had told Bentley's lawyer to take his father's inheritance and shove it up his cold, dead ass. So his father's interest in Lord's Steel had been absorbed back into the family's multibillion-dollar company. Langston had given up all that money, and that was one of the reasons Butch had never respected him.

"Hell, all he had to do was divorce her. It prob-ably would've made fucking her more fun," Butch had said to thirteen-year-old Zach.

When he told his dad what Butch had said, Langston didn't get angry or vicious.

"Marriage can be a farce, but not in the case of your mother and me. You're going to discover this as you get older," Langston said. "The Lords, we do everything with intensity—love, hate, hold grudges, and chase that one unique woman we can't live without. That's who your mom is for me, and all the money in the world could never make me divorce her. She's mine and I'm hers, and we're going to our graves that way."

Elaine started snoring, and Zach smiled. He'd met a lot of women, but the morning Elaine walked past him at the cemetery, it was as though electricity had rushed through him. When he saw her again the next day, it was game over. He just knew she was the one, and every moment they had spent together had proved him right. She had issues with trust, of course. But he could handle it. Zach had nothing to hide, and he wasn't a fucking liar, either. She would trust him one day soon. He was sure of it.

When they made it to his condo, he carried her through the lobby and up his private elevator. He couldn't stop smiling for two reasons—she was safe in his arms, and fucking Charlie lived on the sixth floor! As soon as he entered his place, Elaine stirred.

"Are we home?" she whispered.

"Yes," he said, keeping his voice low.

Her eyes opened, her soft lips found his, and they kissed as he carried her to his bed. Then the lovemaking commenced.

CHAPTER 11

*I*t had to be around eleven o'clock in the morning. As soon as they got into bed, Elaine and Zach made love as though making up for lost time. No man had ever made her body and soul feel that way before. The room was still dark because he had been smart enough to hang blackout shades over his large windows. For that, Zach earned another checkmark in her book.

He held her tightly against him. Normally it would have made her squeamish to be held so long by a man, even after making love for as many hours as they had. That, too, was very different for her, but Elaine didn't want to escape him.

Then his lips kissed her bare shoulders. "Are you

up?" he asked before grinding his rigid manhood against her ass.

"I am," she said in her heavy morning voice.

Zach grinded her once more before inserting himself inside her from behind. Slow, steady, and indulgent was the pace of his thrusts. His mouth was so near her ear. She felt every inch of him. The moaning. The breathing. The whispers of pleasure. Then he sparked something inside her, after making love over and over again before they fell asleep. She knew that if she said, "Ah, there," he would stimulate that spot. He seemed to have already learned her body. In and out he shifted, relying on her sounds to guide him.

"Ah," she cried, uninhibited, and he nailed her in that spot until the orgasm passed.

Then he flipped her over on her back, reentered her, kissed, sucked, and plunged in and out of her until he exploded. Of course, Zach wasn't done. He said he loved to hear and feel her come, so he went down on her until her legs couldn't stop shaking. Finally, she had to raise a hand and tell him her body needed to recover.

"I want to take a bath," she said.

He rolled out of bed, drew her a warm bath, and gave her time alone to bathe.

As Elaine sat in the tub, she kept blinking, wondering when she was going to wake up. But the present wasn't merely a wonderful dream. Zach was really happening in her life right now.

The sex…

She sighed deeply. Even if he was just manipulating her, she never had to have sex ever again. After reaching the heights to which they had soared, there was nowhere else to go.

She heard a soft knock on the frosted glass door. She waited for Zach to open it, but he didn't.

"Come in," she said.

She loved that about him too. He was so considerate, always. The door opened, and in he walked, bright-eyed and grinning from ear to ear. He was holding her purse.

"I thought you might want this."

Then she remembered something. "My phone." She tilted her head slightly to the side. "So today, I get to do whatever I want, right?"

His glowing expression turned into slight panic, but she smiled warmly to let him know what he feared wasn't going to happen.

"I'm staying," she said. "But I do need my phone because I'm pretty sure Sonja, Elaine, and Theresa have been trying to call me for hours."

He chuckled. "That's why I brought this to you."

"Is that so?"

"As I said, I know people, and your sister wants to know all about me. But what I want to know is what are you going to say about me?"

She tossed her head back and chuckled. Hell, where was she going to start?

At least Zach didn't wait around, expecting her to answer that question. He fished her phone out of her purse and then kissed her. She recoiled after realizing she had morning breath.

"By the way, do you have a toothbrush?"

"I have them in the guest bathrooms. I'll bring them in. But after your phone call." He winked.

She grinned and waited for him to leave before powering up the phone.

She had hundreds of messages. Most of them were from work, but a lot were from the family members she'd expected to flood her with calls. Strangely, she wasn't ready to think about AMTA. At some point yesterday, when she'd become happier, she had forgotten she owned it.

SONJA HAD ANSWERED ON THE FIRST RING. ELAINE told her every single detail she could remember about the first moments she met Zach. Then, the sex…

"I didn't know my body could do that over and over and over again like that. It's amazing."

Sonja giggled. "I know. Same here with Jay. I mean, could you have imagined that the scrawny little kid who used to be my best friend, and like an annoying little brother to you, could make a girl come that much?"

"TMI, Son," Elaine said. Picturing Sonja and Jay doing it felt so wrong, even though it was so very right. Even when they were kids, it was evident that they were made for each other. Jay had tried to make it happen with her, but their mother had put a bad taste in Sonja's mouth when it came to involvement with the opposite sex. She'd spent years trying to encourage her sister to get out there and date. That was the only way she was going to discover that not all men were a drag. Although, one by one, all Elaine had picked were duds.

Only after Elaine learned Gary had betrayed her and Sonja found love with Jay had Elaine questioned whether she had it wrong all those years and her sister had it right. Three times left at the altar and once scammed by her fiancé? It took way too long for her to call it quits. But just when she had, in walked Zach. *What the hell?*

Elaine and Sonja got Robin and Theresa on the line, and after Elaine told them everything she had relayed to Sonja, they roughly planned Sonja and Jay's marriage ceremony and wanted it to take place the Saturday after next in Elaine's backyard.

Their phone call had lasted an hour and forty-eight minutes. When Elaine realized she was already missing Zach's face, she knew she was in trouble. She drained the tub and got out.

After she wrapped herself in a towel, she went to the separate vanity area and saw a fresh electric toothbrush, a new tube of cinnamon toothpaste, and a fluffy face towel on the counter, clearly just for her. Elaine studied the items while battling the desire to remind herself that she didn't deserve the treatment Zach was giving her.

During those moments when Robin felt like playing the wise young sage, she would say the brain always chooses the sort of misery it's used to. Elaine had always blown off her cousin's words of wisdom. How could someone who always seemed so inert on the inside know anything about how the brain works?

Elaine was starting to realize that Gary and all her other fiancés and past boyfriends had been men she knew would eventually end up hurting her, and she couldn't get out of the cycle of choosing such a guy. Zach was different. Spending time with him had felt like a shock treatment. So instead of worrying about when and how he would eventually show her how insignificant she truly was to him, Elaine took three deep breaths and let her negative feelings go.

She was starving like Marvin, and on top of that, they had only three hours before the Jacques Blanchard concert. So Elaine hurried and brushed her teeth, washed the old makeup off her face, and put on a little of the lipstick and mascara she kept in her purse to make herself look more alive. While studying herself in the mirror, she realized she didn't need the help. Her skin and eyes were glowing. "I guess they were right," she muttered.

"Who was right?" Zach asked.

She jumped.

"Sorry, babe." He walked behind her and wrapped his arms around her. "Didn't mean to startle you."

Did he just call me "babe"?

"Who was right?" he asked again.

She closed her mouth and swallowed. Was she his babe? "Um, people. You know, they would say I wouldn't be so miserable if I were getting fucked regularly. They never thought I heard them, but I did." A veil of sadness had overtaken her.

"Ah, babe, I'm sorry." He turned her around to face him then kissed her tenderly. "I'd love to talk to you more about that, but my mother's here."

Elaine hinged her neck forward as her jaw dropped. "Your mother?"

None of her past fiancés' mothers had ever liked her, at least not until after she bought them expensive gifts or gave them loans they never intended to repay.

"I know you're nervous about meeting Sarah."

"Is that her name?"

His smile wavered. "Yes."

"It's okay. I'll be fine."

"I know you will. But my mother never shows up unannounced unless there's a reason." He scratched his cheek.

She frowned. "Is everything okay?"

"You need to hear what she has to say."

Elaine pressed a hand on her chest. "Me?"

"Yes. Both of us."

Elaine touched the base of her tight throat then nodded. "Okay," she barely said.

SARAH WATCHED ELAINE AS THOUGH SHE WERE slowly picking her apart. The examination made the hairs stand up on the back of Elaine's neck. She reminded herself that even if Zach's mother didn't like her at first sight, it was not going to kill her.

One look at Sarah's raven hair, porcelain skin, and soft features, and it was easy to see who Zach got his looks from. Sarah didn't look old enough to be his mother. Elaine had lived in LA long enough to spot plastic surgery from a mile way. Without ever being cut, stuck, or filled, Sarah didn't look many years over the age of thirty-five.

When Elaine got close enough, Sarah stood, and they shook hands.

"Hi, I'm Sarah," Zach's mother said.

"I'm Elaine."

They smiled at each other, but Sarah regarded her with a penetrating gaze.

"You're very young to be so accomplished," Sarah said. Her earnest smile told Elaine that impressed her.

Elaine looked down and blushed. "Thank you."

Sarah waited until Elaine lifted her head and said, "I'm sorry to barge in on you both, but when I read this, I had to come over."

Sarah was holding an envelope addressed to her, but there wasn't a return address.

They sat on the sofa, and Zach read the letter out loud. The message was short and to the point. The writer said he or she was a doctor Butch Benjamin had secretly seen. The doctor had never diagnosed Butch with cancer, but Butch had reported symptoms of poisoning. Tests were performed two days before Butch's death. The results came in on Wednesday, and Butch had ingested low doses of cyanide over an extended period of time.

Butch was aware there was a strong chance he had been poisoned, and he'd promised to be cautious. But there wasn't enough poison in his system to cause death between the time he was tested and when he died. The doctor believed a fatal dose had been administered.

Sarah gazed off. "Even when he was a child, Levi insisted on being up to no good." She faced Zach. "I used to be so afraid you'd end up working for or with him somehow. Langston convince me that my brother might be a parasite, but he loved you too much to put you in harm's way." She snarled as she shook her head. "I can't believe he passed on his criminal empire to you. Get rid of it." She shook her head. "And Zach, don't delay. And you"—she turned her attention to Elaine—"I am so sorry, but if my brother had anything to do with your business, then you need to be very careful. Both of you."

CHAPTER 12

They had to cancel their concert plans and get on a flight back to LA. While she was taking a bath, he had instructed his accountant to transfer the thirty-nine shares to Elaine. But Zach asked if he could hold off on completing the transaction because he didn't want to put her in danger.

Elaine's first inclination was to reassure him that he didn't need to worry about her. She could handle Butch's foes and anyone else who wanted to attack her.

"I know you're capable," Zach said, watching her go through her thought process as he sat across from her. "But please allow me to make sure you're safe."

Her frown intensified. It took every fiber of her being to trust Zach enough to nod. "But who do you think poisoned Butch?"

"I don't know. The list of possible suspects is longer than my arm."

One face had been stuck in Elaine's head for the longest. "The person who had the most to gain, and lived the closest to him, was Betsy. After our tête-à-tête in the back seat of her car, I'm a hundred percent sure she's capable of killing her husband."

He closed his eyes and rubbed the middle of his forehead. "She is definitely the obvious culprit, at least on paper. How about we go pay her a visit as soon as we're in LA? And Elaine…"

She raised her eyebrows. "Yes?"

"I would like for you to stay with me until we get some answers."

"Stay with you? What do you mean by that?"

"You'll live at my house until all this is sorted."

She pushed a hand at him dismissively. "I'll be fine in—"

"Elaine. We'll go to your place. You'll pack a bag, and then you'll come stay with me. I won't take no for an answer." He watched her with unwavering focus.

Elaine pursed her lips. Deep down inside, she

hadn't wanted to reject Zach's offer in the first place. She had been waiting for her objections to his proposition to rise to the surface, but they remained suppressed by her intense desire to stay near him.

"Okay," she finally said.

His eyes danced. "Did I hear 'okay'?"

She answered with a small nod.

The fire in his eyes made her simper.

"So, Laney," he said.

She quickly looked up.

"My mom likes you, but more importantly, she respects you."

"But she doesn't know me. Hell, you don't really know me."

He narrowed an eye. "Try me."

"What do you mean?"

"Are you ready?"

"Ready for what?"

"Ready for me to tell you who I suspect you are?"

Elaine hesitated. What if who he thought she was happened to be the awful truth? No one liked her, at least not for real. And spending time with him had been one of the only moments in her life when she was truly happy.

"I won't start until you give me permission. But

I want to remind you of my promise that I'll *never* hurt you."

She closed her eyes and sighed firmly. "Let's hear it," she whispered.

"You're protective of those you love, and people in general, but especially those you believe are unable to protect themselves. Although your grandmother raised you, your mother and father weren't around to protect and love you. So at a young age, you decided to protect not only yourself but also your sister and your cousins. I saw what you did last night."

Elaine felt woozy. "What did I do?"

"You let your sister win the third game."

"No, I didn't," she said, knowing her objection was feeble.

"Laney, you'd been making shots like the one you missed all night long. You didn't want your sister to lose because you didn't want to upset her. But the next time you play her, babe, win."

Elaine had to remember to breathe as inspiration rushed through her body. For the first time ever, she was determined to beat Sonja at their next pool match. "Shit, you're right. I always hated seeing that look on her face when…" She closed her eyes again, trying to banish a painful memory.

"I'm safe, Laney. Say it."

She took a long, jittery sigh. "My mother loved finding losers to be in relationships with. One night, I was awakened by her boyfriend at the time. He was trying to force himself on me, and I fought like hell. I kneed him in the balls and gouged his eyes. My mom had this iron horse in my room, and I clocked him over the head with it, and he lost consciousness. My sister..."

The tears started rolling down her face. "All I could think about was her, wondering if he tried the same thing with Sonja. When I ran into her room, she wasn't in her bed. I just kept screaming her name as loudly as I could, and she opened the closet door. She was safe. She hugged me so tight. She was shaking. She said she heard the boogeyman walking in the hallway and ran and hid in her closet. I was twelve, and she was seven, and I remember thinking no one in my school went through the shit we had to go through with our mom. At least they didn't look like it. But what if he had succeeded with her?" Elaine broke down at the thought of her little sister, whom she loved so much, experiencing something so horrible.

When Elaine opened her eyes, Zach was unclipping her seat belt, then he took her by the hands and led her to stand. She rose to her feet. He sat down in her chair and guided her onto his lap.

"Sorry, I didn't mean to make you sad."

She sniffed and was embarrassed by her sniveling. "The past is in the past, so…"

"You know that's not true, Laney. Our pasts make us who we are right now. And hell, you fought him. I knew the moment I met you that you were a fighter."

Elaine tried to smile at the thought of that one person who had always made life worth living. "Our grandmother taught us how to fight."

Zach used a cloth napkin to wipe her face then held it to her nose. "Blow."

Elaine recoiled at first. She was not a child, and the crying made her appear weaker than she was. But Zach was only being loving, supportive, and gentle, so she blew. She could also feel that Zach had grown firm beneath her. They started kissing slowly but intensely. With each stroke of the tongue and caressing of the lips, Elaine felt as though her heart would burst.

He took off her shirt. He unclipped her bra and devoured her breasts, growing even harder beneath her. She could feel her body recline backward with the chair. Soon Elaine was lying on her back. Zach took off her shoes then tugged her pants off. His pants came off. She parted her knees to receive him, and he gave her all of him.

———

Zach wanted to make her climax until the airplane landed, but she was starving, so they remained naked while lying together under a duvet. They sat up long enough to eat prime rib, new potatoes, and glazed carrots, but then they lowered their seat again.

With her head on his chest, she told Zach things she'd never told anyone—not Gran, Sonja, or any man she had been engaged to. Zach now knew that she was a product of infidelity. Her father was married when her mother had gotten pregnant, and Carrie Anne had tried to use her pregnancy to make Elaine's father divorce his wife and marry her. Carrie Anne had even stalked her father's wife and confessed that she was having his baby. The woman laughed in Carrie Anne's face and called her garbage.

"Have you ever met your father?" Zach asked.

"Yes, but Sonja has more to do with him than me. I hate the guy."

"Because you did what you felt was his job. You protected your sister."

Not until that very moment had she realized that. All she knew was that whenever Luke came around, she wanted to rip his face off with her teeth. That was how much anger and hate he inspired within her.

"But I can look at your mom and tell your parents were perfect, weren't they?" she asked.

Zach paused. "No one's perfect."

"It's okay to admit it, Zach. I won't feel bad."

"I meant it. My parents couldn't be perfect because no human being can be. And hell, what does perfect mean, anyway? If perfect means not hurting others for the sake of ego, then yeah, they were perfect. But they communicated a lot. They listened to each other. They listened to me."

"My gran listened to me too."

He kissed her on top of her head. "I can't wait to meet Lorraine Hester in the flesh. How are you going to introduce me?"

She could feel he was smiling.

Elaine chuckled. "How do you want to be introduced?"

"I want to give this a go, for real. No fucking around. You're with me. I'm with you. Not to sound like we're in high school, but let's go steady."

She laughed. "Steady?"

"I'll let you wear my letterman's jacket and class ring. Did they do that in high school in LA?"

"Only the corny kids."

He laughed. They kissed and were about to get hot and heavy, as usual.

"Law," she whispered.

His fingers were sinking in and out of her. "Huh?"

"I love practicing the law. That's what I should be doing."

He stopped stimulating her. Apparently her confession had wakened him out of his lustful daze. "That's a long way from running agents."

Elaine's next thought made her squeeze her eyes as tightly as she could. "I made a mistake. I don't want the company. Keep the shares." When she opened her eyes, he was staring into them.

"I'm going to give you all of your shares, and we're going to get all your money back and more."

She shook her head adamantly. "I don't need three billion dollars. I never wanted it."

"Elaine, that doesn't make sense."

She explained how she'd invested in ConnectUp

and told him how depressed she was when she learned how much money she'd earned. Then she explained the reason for her despair, which was something else she had been too embarrassed to divulge. "I just believed real men didn't want women who were so rich and powerful, not without wanting to bring them down to the right size. I figured I'd rather already not be a threat to their egos." She shook her head. "Now that I'm saying it out loud, it sounds insane and weak."

"Being weak is easy. Being truly strong is hard to achieve. But you've achieved it. So don't ever apologize for it."

Elaine's lips parted so that she could release a caught breath.

"And at this point, who gives a fuck about what any other guy wants from you," he continued. "I like you the way you are. You're sharp, ambitious, shrewd, and tough. But you're also vulnerable and empathetic." He smirked. "You can be tough on those you thought were hurtful. You fired sixty-seven agents in less than a month."

Elaine frowned. "How did you know that? I never told you that."

"Allison told me."

"Well…" She stopped herself from saying they

deserved it. Then she groaned. "Oh gosh. I'm such a bitch."

"No, you're not." He kissed her forehead. "No, you're not." Now her lips. "No, you're not."

They were kissing again. Her head was floating in the stratosphere. Zach was ready and wanting round two. This time, Elaine gave him a treat. She put him in her mouth until he lifted her off her knees, rolled her on her back, and sank himself inside her.

CHAPTER 13

THREE HOURS LATER

It was seven in the evening, but the sun hadn't set. Betsy lived in the kind of Beverly Hills neighborhood where everyone expected Gran to live. However, Gran always said she needed to make her life somewhere that reminded her of the journey from runaway to having her own successful real estate firm. The house in Hancock Park had gone through so many modernizing renovations over the years. Millions were pumped into that property instead of purchasing a new one because of the memories the house had stored within.

Betsy Benjamin's mansion was built in the classic Spanish Colonial style. The lawn was bright green, adorned by beautifully pruned and flowering tropical trees. The roof was of red brick, and the façade of the house featured arches. Zach had tried to call Betsy twice after he and Elaine had made love and fifteen minutes before landing, but both calls went straight to voicemail. A half hour later, Elaine tried, and the widow answered on the third ring. Elaine told her that she had spoken to Zach and they had reached an agreement.

"What is it?" Betsy abrasively asked.

"I would like to share the details in person."

"No. What is it?"

"Yes. Or you can forget about it and I can rene-gotiate with him. Call me if you decide to see things my way. I'll give you ten minutes."

"No need," Betsy said without pause. Then she gave Elaine her address.

"You just got me hard," Zach said as they got into his SUV.

Elaine laughed. It felt good to know he appreci-ated her effective hard-ass side. Now, however, she realized that was more like a superpower to use only when necessary and never to kick anyone when they were already down. People. That was what watching Zach had taught her was important. It was time she saw far beneath the surface of people.

Zach said he wasn't familiar with Betsy's address. He could attest that as far he knew, Butch had never lived there. However, the plan was to shock Betsy into an extreme reaction by having Zach accompany Elaine. For the second time, they rang the doorbell. The neighborhood's gate guard had confirmed that Betsy was home and expecting them. Perhaps she had seen Zach through a window and decided against meeting with Elaine.

"Do you hear that?" Zach asked, inclining his ear toward the door.

Elaine stood very still, then she heard it. "It sounds like a small dog barking."

"Stay close to me," Zach said.

She nodded and followed him along the front of the house as they moved toward the barking. Before they could reach the back of the house, a fluffy white dog came running toward them. It kept jumping up on Zach's legs.

"It's Fifi," Zach said and picked up the animal.

"Is she Betsy's pet?" Elaine asked.

He frowned as if he was gargling with vinegar.

"I don't know. I saw the dog at the house a few times, but Butch said it didn't belong to her. He never liked living with animals."

"Then whose pet is she?"

"I don't know. That was then, this is now. Betsy probably found a way to keep her." His brows ruffled more as he slowly examined both ends of the large house. "Something's wrong. I'm going to need you to follow me to the car and wait there."

She leaned away from him. "Um, no, Zach. I'm going into the house with you."

"We don't have time to argue. But I'm going to get my weapon. And you stay in the car with fucking Fifi."

"What if something happens to you?" she asked.

"As long as nothing happens to you, I'll be fine."

Elaine heaved a sigh as she looked at the tiny animal shivering in her arms and watching her with big helpless eyes.

"All right," she said. "I'll wait in the car with Fifi." Plus, she didn't want to be one of those stupid and impossible women that she had read about in bad TV and film scripts. Obviously something had gone very wrong if Fifi, who looked like a pampered little princess, was running free in the yard and barking, with Betsy nowhere in sight.

She had now been sitting in the car for seven minutes. The windows were up, air-conditioning on, doors locked, and engine running. Fifi had stopped barking and was staring out the window as though she could see what was happening through the walls of the house. Suddenly, two squad cars came to a screeching halt behind Zach's SUV. Then an ambulance came blaring down the tree-lined street behind them. No way was Elaine going to continue sitting in the car. She quickly turned off the engine, took the keys and the dog with her, and went to see what in the hell was going on.

"Excuse me, Officers," she called, running up the lawn while trying to keep her heels from sinking into the grass.

"Did you call us, ma'am?" asked one of the two burly men in short-sleeved dark-blue uniforms.

"No, I believe my boyfriend did. He's inside. I can take you to him."

At first they seemed hesitant, but when the EMTs started running in their direction, one of them said, "Show us."

It was quite a run to the edge of the house,

along the side, then around to the back. The large French doors opened into a living room decorated with traditional English furniture. Although Elaine was breathing heavily, she felt her heart stop at the sight of Betsy lying on the floor while Zach performed CPR.

Fifi was yapping again, and Elaine tried petting her some more to calm her. It didn't work. The dog was now trying to jump out of her arms, but Elaine tapped her collar and said, "Stay." Fifi kept barking but stopped struggling.

The paramedics took over for Zach, who told them she had a weak pulse but was still alive.

"Treat her for acute cyanide poisoning," Zach added as though it was a sudden afterthought. "She was alive three hours ago."

One of the EMTs frowned dubiously.

"Her husband, who died last week, was poisoned by cyanide. She has no abrasions or gunshot wounds. Treat her. Test her. It could be a matter of life and death."

"Let's get her out of here, stat." The frowning EMT nodded once at Zach. "Thanks for the report."

The remaining officers asked them questions

about what had happened when they arrived and specifics about the call Elaine had with Betsy earlier.

"It looked like she had a heart attack," one of the officers said.

"But the back door was open, and the dog was out," Elaine said.

The officer studied her as though he were seeing her for the first time. "I understand, ma'am, but people let their dogs out in the backyard all the time. As of now, there's no evidence of foul play, but we'll keep an eye on her progress."

Elaine was about to insist they collect some evidence when Zach put a hand on her waist.

"Do you have any further questions for us?" he asked.

"No, but we'll be in touch," the officer said.

"Thank you," Zach said and shook his hand.

They were able to remain in the home because Zach was Betsy's nephew. He called Linus, her son, and told him what had happened. Linus said he would go straight to the hospital.

Elaine and Zach stood in the living room. She noticed how untouched everything was. It was certainly not a room that was used much.

"Do you really think she was poisoned?" Elaine asked.

"I do." Zach sounded certain of it. Then he searched in one direction of the house then the other.

"What is it?" she asked.

Zach pressed a finger against her lips, signaling her to be quiet. He put his mouth next to her ear. "Follow me."

That was when Elaine knew he suspected the house was bugged. She followed him down the hallway while still holding Fifi. He stopped abruptly at the door of a sitting room, where a wineglass sat next to a dessert plate that had crumbs on top.

Zach walked over, sniffed the glass, and shook his head, signaling there was nothing off about the smell. Then he used a cloth napkin to run his hand under the cocktail table. He did the same to the chairs and around the shelves of a large console. He picked up the lamp, then he turned and looked over his shoulder and across the room at a world globe made of glass. He walked over and picked up the ball off the gold base then put it back down.

He pointed his head toward the hallway and mouthed, "Come with me."

ZACH SAID HE SAW A VOICE TRANSMITTER IN THE base of the globe. He knew that for certain because he'd developed a company that manufactured a chip required in all voice-transmission technologies. Its sole purpose was range control, but the chip also gave law enforcement agencies other capabilities, like signal tracking.

When they stepped out of the house, Zach called Corliss Laboratory to come over to Betsy's and unlock the mysteries of the electronic bug. After Fifi relieved herself in the backyard, they all waited in the SUV for the technology experts to arrive. Elaine and Zach were trying to figure out why someone would want Betsy dead.

"It seems so random, especially since she was left with nothing, really," Elaine said. "She strikes me as a shrewd Beverly Hills housewife who wants restitution after being married to a man who humiliated her for so many years by having multiple affairs with low-grade ass."

Zach grunted thoughtfully then scratched the side of his face. "I think Betsy was on the board of directors, though."

"Of Butch's company."

"Yes."

She twisted her mouth. "Humph."

"Betsy was not the sort who overdid it at the gym and on Rodeo Drive. What you experienced of her at the funeral was classic Betsy, babe."

Elaine tensed up. He'd called her that a number of times, and in every instance, it had gone unaddressed.

"So, you're calling me 'babe' these days," she said.

"Does it bother you? If so, then I'll wait until you're comfortable with it."

"I'm comfortable," she said quickly. "But we've just gone so fast, you know..."

He scratched his brow impatiently, searching the rearview mirror. "We're adults, Elaine. We go as fast or as slow as we fucking want to go."

"You're right."

Finally, Zach glanced over, wearing her favorite smirk. "We're right for each other." He opened the car door. "They're here."

Once they were inside, the technician was able to detect three devices. One was in the study, one was in Betsy's bedroom, and of course there was the one in the base of the globe. He then used a device that disturbed the radio waves enough to make them active but unable to pick up and transmit sound. As soon as that process was complete, they were allowed to talk again.

"This was a pretty sophisticated setup, and the transmitters are top-of-the-line," the technician said. He used a tiny tool with sharp ends to delicately pick at the device inside the globe's base. Finally, he extracted a tiny chip and inserted it into a slot within a square machine he'd brought with him. After performing a series of diagnostics, he directed their attention to an electronic map that showed where the voice recordings were being sent.

"What's the address?" Zach asked.

The technician tapped a series of buttons on his screen then told them the address.

"Wait. I know that address. What was it again?" Elaine asked.

The technician repeated it.

Elaine's throat felt so tight that she could hardly speak. "This isn't good, Zach. I need to make a phone call."

"Who do you need to call?"

Elaine rummaged in her purse for her cell

phone. "The person who helped me before. She's your cousin, actually. At least, I think she is. Maggie Adams."

Zach frowned. "Whose address is it?"

Elaine took a steadying breath and told him.

CHAPTER 14

*M*aggie Adams had once given Elaine a private number where she or someone on her team could always be reached. When Elaine called it, Maggie was not available, but someone was still sent to Betsy's house to start an investigation.

Everything happened so fast from that point on. The globe was put back on its base with the listening device still deactivated. The police were back. It was confirmed that Betsy had been poisoned. Unfortunately, she had died. It broke Zach's heart, and now he was more determined than ever to find the killer.

The address that was receiving the signal from the bug was that of a club owned by Gary, Elaine's ex-fiancé. What Elaine loved about Maggie's team was how fast they got shit done. They were able to walk, chew gum, and shoot a gun at the same time.

The male agent, Number One, was extremely muscular and exactly Zach's height. The woman, Number Seven, was tall and, like Maggie, resembled a supermodel. As with the last time Elaine had worked with Maggie's team, they wouldn't reveal their names to her, but they had all been assigned numbers.

The two agents had a security clearance that obviously made the police department willing to work with them. They directed the evidence collection. All the gathered fingerprints were analyzed in a van parked in the long driveway. The brawny guy questioned Elaine and Zach extensively about the people involved in Butch's business and the activities that had transpired regarding AMTA since Butch had died. They were given the names of Allison Johnson, all the people Elaine had fired on Thursday, the sixty-seven agents she had fired, and of course, Mike Falk.

Number One focused on Zach. "What you did with the recording devices, good thinking. You discovered them. We've got the serial numbers and models. You've put us in a favorable position to get this resolved very soon."

Zach folded his arms. "How soon is very soon?"

"Step off the premises. Let us complete our investigation, and we'll give you a call when it's over."

Zach grunted. His smirk was more sarcastic than usual.

Number One nodded graciously. "I know it's difficult to leave it in our hands. But I promise, we're able to get further and faster than most. We're here to help *you*, Mr. Lord and Ms. Hester."

After an intense pause, Zach took a step back. "Okay. I'll get us somewhere safe and wait to hear from you."

Number One shook his hand and then Elaine's, then he quickly walked away from them. They had let Fifi relieve herself one more time before loading up in Zach's car and heading to his house in Malibu.

He had decided to drive them directly to his place without stopping by her house first so that she could pack some things. It was late, and he thought it would be better to head to her house sometime tomorrow, during daylight.

Zach had remained stoic after basically telling

her the plans he had made for her, not asking. As the seconds passed, Elaine wanted to blow her top and demand he take her to Robin's, Theresa's, or even Gran's for the night. But he was right about the danger she was in, and the worst thing she could do was put her family in any danger.

Elaine knew exactly why she wanted to run away from Zach. All day yesterday and earlier today, he had been so vivacious and lighthearted, but now it was as if he were trapped in a black cloud. She had to remind herself that internalizing his mood was immature. He'd learned his uncle was poisoned. Then he had to administer CPR to his aunt, who later died. He shouldn't have to play Prince Charming in order to make her feel secure.

"Elaine," he said out of the blue.

She jumped. "Yes."

"Sorry, didn't mean to startle you." He reached over and took the hand that wasn't petting Fifi. "Didn't you say a go-go dancer had set up your —the guy?"

Elaine was relieved to know what he had been pondering all this time. "Yes. I forgot her name, though, but yes."

He rubbed his chin. "Humph. Butch kept a

healthy stream of strippers, hookers, go-go dancers, and shit."

Zach made a quick right turn into a grocery store parking lot, and after a series of other turns, they were heading in the opposite direction, traveling on the Pacific Coast Highway.

"Where are you going?"

"Butch's house. I know where he keeps a key."

Elaine pointed at the glove compartment. "Are you going to need that?"

"What do you mean by that?"

"Your gun. Do you always keep it in your car?"

"Yes, I always keep a weapon close," he said. He told her a story of a number of successful businessmen who had endured attempted kidnappings.

It made sense. She knew what Zach Lord was worth, and it was way more than Gran's net worth.

"But don't worry, babe. I'm very proficient in using my weapon."

She cut a smile. From his tone, she was sure the double entendre was intended.

"Unless you know otherwise," he said.

Elaine turned to look at him. He glanced at her with his sexy smirk.

"I would say your weapons are extremely proficient," she crooned.

"Only proficient?"

"You're an expert, actually."

When she looked at him again, he was smiling. It felt good to know she played a part in lightening his mood.

"So what are we looking for in Butch's house?" she asked to direct their minds on other things besides what they had been doing a lot of lately.

"Phone numbers, receipts, anything that's directly related to Butch's sexual lifestyle. He was into a lot of vulgar shit."

"Not surprised," Elaine said.

"And on another note, I was also thinking you should keep your company even after I return the shares to you."

"Oh yeah? Why?"

"There's no way you're going to recover what you paid at this juncture, but over time, we'll be able to get your money back. TV, films, sporting events, they're all consumer staples, babe."

"I know. They're products people choose not to live without. But I just want to get rid of the biggest mistake I ever made."

"I think you're making an emotional decision here. Don't get me wrong, emotions shouldn't be discounted, but neither should rationality. Three billion dollars? No one gives away that kind of cash and gets nothing in return. It's not smart. It's not good business."

Elaine groaned and sighed. "I know it's not good business. But you're the one who took me on this weekend trip through Wonderland. I gathered the theme was live free and choose happiness. Right?"

"But I'm at your disposal. We're going to do this together. And you don't have to steer the ship and own the company. We can get someone else to do that. Someone who knows how to rebuild your business and—"

The console rang, signaling a new caller. The name Linus was on the screen. Zach immediately answered.

"Linus, hey, buddy. I'm sorry to hear about your mother."

"Where the fuck is my dog?" he shouted.

Elaine and Zach looked at each other in surprise then down at Fifi in her lap.

"She's with us. She's safe," Zach said calmly.

"My mom has been fucking murdered. I want my dog, and I want her right now." Clearly Zach's tone did little to put Linus back on the hinges.

"Well, we're busy right now, but—"

"Where are you?" he snapped. "I want Fifi."

Zach frowned intensely. "I'm aware of that, Linus. But we're driving up the canyon. On our way to Butch's."

"Don't you fucking remember I live near Butch? I'll be there in a minute." He ended the call.

Zach looked at Elaine with raised eyebrows.

She shrugged. "He lost his mother. Maybe that's an excuse."

He nodded as if he agreed with her. "They were unnaturally close."

"I've heard of sons dying shortly after their mothers pass. It's called maternal emotional incest."

Zach muttered something, but it sounded as though he agreed with her. Since they were on a winding, private mountain road that led to the gates of Butch's property, he pulled over and waited for Linus.

"He doesn't need to be on the property with us," Zach said.

Zach stared at the windshield at first. Elaine was beginning to welcome the silence when he faced her.

"By the way, how are you doing in there with all that's going on?" He pointed at her heart.

She smiled tightly. "I'm doing well. Thanks for asking."

"I couldn't have predicted having a day like this, especially after last night and our flight."

There he went, flirting with his eyes again.

"Me neither. But we may not find anything in Butch's home. Are you prepared for that?"

His smirk was slight. "I promise, if we find nothing, I'll leave the detective work to the… What are they, anyway? Number One and Number Seven?"

Elaine chuckled. "Good question. I think they're secret agents. They have access to technology and equipment that can perform magic."

"Humph," he said, nodding thoughtfully. "This Maggie must be Jack and Charlie's cousin by marriage. There were no girls born in the Lord family."

"Oh," Elaine said.

They ended up grinning at each other again. Her heart started palpitating, and so did her nether regions. Zach had accomplished the difficult feat of making her horny at the drop of a hat.

"As soon as we hand Fifi off, I want your jeans off and you sitting on my lap," he said with desire burning in his eyes.

All Elaine could do was gnaw on her bottom lip to keep her lust contained.

Then he took her by the side of her face and guided her mouth to his. She loved kissing Zach, and she could tell he enjoyed it just the same. Their mouths stayed engaged until a white SUV soared past them then screeched to a halt.

Suddenly Fifi piped up, as though she knew her master was in the vicinity.

Zach frowned at the vehicle as though he didn't recognize it, then a guy got out of the passenger seat and stood behind it.

"It's Linus. Come on, Fifi," Zach said as he picked her up off Elaine's lap.

The dog started barking and clawing to stay with Elaine.

"I know, I wouldn't want to leave her either," he said.

Their eyes flirted with each other, then Zach got out of the driver's seat and slammed the door behind him. Through the illumination of the headlights, Elaine could see that Linus had a small build, but he was dressed like someone out for a night on the town, not a guy who had rushed to the hospital to see his dying mother. Then her gaze fell on Zach, who was a remarkable specimen of a man compared to his scrawnier step-cousin. Fifi kept barking and squirming as Zach continued to make his approach. In a matter of seconds or minutes, Zach's erection would be inside her yet again. Recalling the pleasure made her shift her right leg a little toward the door. When her foot touched her purse, she felt her phone vibrating inside.

"Damn it," she said and hurried to fish out her device, thinking it must be Sonja, Theresa, or perhaps Gran calling to see if their flight landed safely. But the number on the screen took her by surprise.

"Hello," she said after quickly tapping the answer button.

"Elaine, this is Number Seven." It was the woman. "I know you're with Zach. Is Linus with you now?"

"Yes, he's taking Fifi."

"Do not engage him. We have confirmed that he poisoned his mother and more than likely Butch as well."

Elaine threw her body forward to get a better look at the scene. She saw a third guy, who was pointing what appeared to be a gun at Zach, whose hands were up. Linus was holding Fifi, who was still barking her head off.

"The guy has a gun," Elaine said. She immediately threw the phone on the seat.

Zach, Linus, and the other guy turned to look in her direction. There wasn't even a question of what to do next, and she needed to act fast. Elaine retrieved Zach's gun out of the glove compartment. Her hands wanted to shake and drop the weapon, but she forced them to remain steady. Suddenly, she saw Linus walking toward her vehicle. There was no way he could make it to the SUV before she got out.

Elaine finally flipped the safety and quickly stepped out of the vehicle, pointing the gun at Linus's head.

"If he takes him, I take you!" she shouted.

Linus stopped in his tracks.

Fifi barked and squirmed. Now she knew why the dog had been so expressive since Linus's arrival.

"Shoot me, then," he said.

Elaine knew he believed she was only bluffing. She didn't like guns, but that didn't mean she didn't know how to use one. Without a second thought, she pulled the trigger. A shot rang out, and Linus shrieked as he fell on the knee that had hot metal in it.

Sirens blared. Another gun shot rang out, but it

hadn't come from her weapon. Zach was rolling on the ground with the other gunman.

Elaine was the kind of shooter who always hit the center of the target, but she didn't want to take the shot because it was too dark. Fifi was behind her, barking. Elaine kept her weapon trained on Linus, who was rolling around on the ground, crying in pain.

Number Seven and Number One arrived, and together they had jumped into Zach's tussle with the gunman. Within seconds, he was on his stomach and handcuffed.

Another squad car arrived. The officers got out, taking cover behind their door with their weapons drawn and aimed at Elaine, who quickly dropped Zach's gun and held her hands up in the air.

"Get your fucking guns off of her," Number Seven shouted. Now! Off of her! Now!"

The officers hesitated but did as she said.

Number Seven pointed her gun at Linus, who was rolling around on the ground in agony because of the hot lead in his kneecap. "Get him in cuffs. He's our suspect, and he's under arrest."

Then she was on her cell phone, calling for an ambulance.

SUNDAY MORNING

Zach and Elaine slept hard. After the last two days, they were wiped. But Elaine was awakened by the sound of her cell phone ringing. It was Maggie Adams, who had called to give her a complete report on their case. Zach woke up shortly thereafter, and they sat up in bed with the speakerphone on, listening.

The security guard on duty at the gates of Betsy's neighborhood during the timeframe of her poisoning had said a woman named Tory Antler was granted entrance around three thirty in the afternoon. Antler worked at Gary's club and was also a high-end call girl who had customers in the neighborhood. She often entered and left under a veil of secrecy, which was why her name wasn't written in the log.

Antler had been arrested and her car seized. Linus's prints were found in the trunk. He was the one who had given his mother the globe as a gift, and his prints were also found on the bug. Investigators knew for a fact that Linus was the one who'd poisoned his mother because they were able to use their equipment to recover the recordings from the company hired to monitor and store what was collected from the listening devices. The authorities were able to obtain conversations dated at least a month before Butch's death.

Before Betsy was murdered, she was drinking tea when her son plainly told her that he was going to kill her and no one would suspect him. His mother had responded with disbelief. When she realized he was serious, she tried to yell for help, but he had subdued her then injected her with a lethal dose of cyanide poison.

However, Maggie informed them, Betsy was by no means innocent. She and Linus were behind the poisoning of Butch, who was one of Tory Antler's clients. She was paid a lot of money to microdose him with cyanide over a period of time so that he would feel sick enough to make an appointment with his doctor, which he had done. Butch's doctor's office had referred him to a crooked oncologist, who had falsely diagnosed him with cancer. The worker who made the referral was paid to do so and had been arrested and questioned.

"What about Michael Falk?" Zach asked.

"We have no evidence that he was involved with

their scheme. As a matter of fact, I have sufficient evidence to suggest otherwise."

She explained that after going through recordings and questioning Mike Falk and others, they had learned Linus played a prominent role in working with Archie Rubenstein to take over AMTA. Butch had found out three weeks ago and given Linus seven days to resign from his position. Betsy had sided with Butch. Then after Butch's murder, Linus tried to convince his mother to have the board reinstate him as company president, but she basically told him to go to hell. But not because she thought what her son had done was wrong. She had planned to sell BLB to the company's competitor, the Carter Group, and one of two things had to happen before that deal was sealed: either she could convince Zach to hand over what was rightfully hers, or she would off him.

"Kill me?" Zach asked.

"Yes." Maggie sounded way too pragmatic about it. Elaine guessed it was because she was familiar with the backstabbing and murder necessary to ascend the throne of power.

Maggie explained that her agents had concluded Linus heard the conversation between Elaine and his mother yesterday. After their phone call ended, Betsy immediately placed another call to a man named Heinrich Forster of Carter Group. She told him it appeared as though Zach Lord had seen the light and they'd be closing the deal sooner than suspected, and without all the mess and fuss they had predicted.

"And you're positive Mike wasn't in on any of it?" Zach asked.

"I'm positive. He wanted you to return the shares to the original shareholders so Linus's actions wouldn't come back to bite BLB in the ass. He thought it would be best to let you, Elaine, duke it out with the original shareholders for control of AMTA."

Zach gazed off with an intense frown. "I'll give Mike a call, then."

Elaine could tell her new boyfriend was glad Mike hadn't been as crooked as the others.

"So Linus and Tory Antler are going up for murder. Forster and others are still under investigation."

"Oh, what about Fifi?" Elaine asked. She had fallen in love with the pretty pooch and hoped to be able to give her a new home.

"Fifi has been claimed by Linus's wife, Ophelia," Maggie said. "The pet was her animal.

According to Ophelia, Linus punished her by hiding Fifi and told her he wouldn't return the animal until he wasn't pissed off at her anymore. By all accounts, Linus was a typical sociopath."

"I bought his good-guy act hook, line, and sinker," Zach said.

"That's why the good-boy-and-girl acts are so effective," Maggie remarked.

They all fell silent for a few beats.

"Maggie, I sincerely thank you for coming through for me, for us"—Elaine rubbed Zach's shoulder—"yet again."

"My pleasure," she said.

"And I'll take care of the bill," Zach said.

"No way," Maggie insisted. "Lords receive our service free of charge. It's a perk of being part of the family. Welcome, Zach."

Zach quickly faced Elaine. She loved seeing him grin and turn red.

"Thanks for the welcome, Maggie."

"Can't wait to meet you. And Elaine, I guess I'll see you at your house in a few weeks. I've received Sonja's pop-up email invitation. It's quite, well, an interesting way of inviting someone to your wedding."

"Don't mind my sister. That's her way of

exerting as little energy as possible while forcing herself to do what she abhors."

Maggie and Elaine laughed. There was no need to inform Maggie that Sonja and Jay were already married and her sister was only going through with a ceremony because she thought it would make everyone else happy. Of course, Elaine had only herself to blame for that. And from that moment on, she promised to work like hell to let her sister and cousins live and let live.

Their call ended, but Elaine and Zach were still gazing into each other's eyes. A bigger conversation was needed regarding AMTA, but they were naked and in bed together and, after the call with Maggie, anxiety free. Last night after they'd left the scene of the crime, Elaine had fallen asleep on the drive to Zach's. She remembered how she walked into his home, with her head leaning on his shoulder. She wanted to express the right sort of reaction at how stunning the place looked, but when Elaine opened her mouth, she yawned. Zach set the alarm system, then they went straight to his room, stripped, and flowed into bed.

Now, bright light was pressing against the tan twill shades covering the floor-to-ceiling windows.

They were grinning at each other, knowing that it was time to make love and then more love.

"Before we get it on"—Elaine grinned coquettishly while rubbing her belly—"we need food for energy. I'm starving."

"Ah, yes, that. Food." He reached over and hit a button on the wall.

"Yes, sir," a voice said.

Zach turned to Elaine. "What do you want to eat, babe? Anything you want, Gee will make it."

She ordered shrimp and grits with home fries. Zach had strawberry crepes with a spinach-and-feta omelet.

"And, um, you know that whipped cream I asked you for?"

"Yes, sir," Gee said.

"We're going to need that now, and the chocolate syrup," Zach said, sliding his fingers up and down Elaine's wetness.

She had no doubt what he was going to use the condiments for. As soon as they arrived, he seasoned the parts of her that he wanted to savor.

CHAPTER 15

THEIR FIRST MONDAY TOGETHER

Zach and Elaine arrived at the office together. After stepping out of the passenger seat of his SUV, she studied her car, which had collected a layer of dust after sitting idle for three days. Her vehicle looked so lonely. It reminded her of how her heart used to feel.

Then she remembered something. "Oh," she said and opened the door she had just closed.

"I have them," Zach said.

When she walked around to him, he was holding the three boxes of homemade doughnuts.

"Are you ready?" he asked.

Elaine took a deep, settling breath and nodded.

"You can do it, babe."

She held her hands out to receive the dough-nuts. "I know."

He smirked and handed over the boxes.

They kissed before walking to the elevator then kissed some more once inside. A lot of changes were planned for the day, but the one challenge Elaine was soon to face was something she'd never done in her professional career.

The elevator doors slid open on the twenty-third floor, and only Elaine got off.

Zach winked at her. "Have fun."

She groaned as she pressed her lips into a tight smile.

"You can do it, babe," he said.

"Thanks, babe," she said. After what they had done yesterday, she felt no uncertainty in referring to him as her babe. She and Zach were full-fledged, making it work, and so far they were getting along swimmingly.

The elevator doors closed, and suddenly she felt strange being out of his presence. They hadn't left each other's side in the last seventy-two hours. But she remembered she had her big-girl panties on. Yes, she could behave like a bitch toward others. That was never a secret to her. She knew she acted that way because she never expected anyone to like her in the first place.

"Who gives a care if someone doesn't like you, Laney? Everybody's not going to like you or, hell, me, either," Zach had said during one of their pillow-talk breaks before making love yet again. "But I like you. I like everything about you."

She tilted her head curiously. "Like what?"

"You're smart as hell. That turns me the fuck on. You have good instincts. You're daring. You're up for anything."

"Well, I let you lead me down a path of debauchery because I wanted my shares."

"Bullshit. You were having too much fun."

She chuckled. "You're right. I was having a fucking blast," she said as loudly as she could and flipped onto her back.

Zach had mounted her and opened her up yet again.

The memory had Elaine smiling from ear to ear as she walked into the operations office. Thinking about how much Zach liked her and, hell, how much she liked the person she saw herself become that weekend had made her mission that much easier.

Elaine gave her employees a dozen of the

doughnuts prepared by Gee, who was an excellent cook, way better than the one she employed at her house. She did exactly as Zach coached her by making a comment about traffic and then asking questions about where everyone lived and about their families. She never thought anyone would want her in their business that way, but they talked about their kids and spouses, and Cesar even told her about the secret office on the sky-deck floor.

"We can get you set up in there today if you want us to," he said.

Elaine beamed, enjoying how nice everyone was to her and not simply because she was the boss. It was because she was the boss and she *cared*.

"What do you think would be the best use of that space?" she asked him.

His eyes grew wide. He was definitely not prepared to be asked that question.

"Listen, next week there'll be a big budget and logistics meeting. I want you there to discuss best practices when it comes to space and how we're using the three floors, including that overindulgent office on the sky-view floor. Are you okay with that?"

"Yeah, sure." He frowned as he nodded. "I'm

kind of overworked here and underpaid as it is, though."

She smiled. "Say no more. I'll have Fiona look into your pay steps and revising your position. I understand things didn't always go so fairly around here. That's changed. So get ready to impress the hell out of us during that meeting, and we'll discuss your pay and job title today, and someone from HR will get back to you in the morning. Deal?"

Cesar smiled in a manner that said he knew he'd respectfully earned what he'd asked for and was finally going to get it. "Deal," he said.

They shook on it.

Elaine walked out of Operations feeling as though she were walking on air. She took the next dozen doughnuts to Accounting and Finance and the final box to Personnel. Those two departments weren't as open to conversation as Operations had been. Still, she didn't take it personally when they didn't want to chitchat. Last Thursday, she had shaken things up around them, big-time. It was going to take a while to get them to trust her, which was something she and Zach had talked about.

The rest of the day was dedicated to the business of letting go. She had officially signed for the thirty-nine shares of AMTA that Zach had promised her. After that, Elaine met with Fiona Meadows and let her know that she officially owned the company one hundred percent and offered her the job of president of AMTA.

Fiona hunched her shoulders and whipped her face sideways, frowning. "Are you serious? Zach Lord gave you the shares?"

"Yes, he did."

"And you want me to be the president and not you?"

Elaine sat up straight. It was time to confess. "First, I should've never bought this company. And second, I should've never tried to run it. It was just that AMTA had the worst fucking agents on the planet, except for you and a handful of others, and I wanted to stick it to them."

"I know," Fiona said, nodding as if she understood exactly what Elaine meant.

"You do?"

"Yes, Laney. You're a goddamn lawyer, not an agent. You fight us. You're not supposed to lead us. Now, granted, we had some of the worst fuckers in the business working here. However, you got rid of them all. So I'd be happy to run this ship for you. What are you going to do in the meantime?"

Elaine took a deep breath. "Okay…" She readjusted in her seat. "So this is where it could get a little sticky for you. And listen, I understand if you change your mind after I—"

"What, Elaine?" Fiona folded her arms over her chest.

"Mega Link Venture Group will be on board as of tomorrow."

"Zach Lord's company? What's up with the two of you, anyway?"

"We're dating."

Fiona slapped a hand over her mouth as she inhaled sharply. "Get the fuck out of here."

Elaine scratched the back of her neck. "We're dating. And actually, it's more than that."

"That was fast."

She shrugged. "I know."

"But you don't do fast."

"I know that too."

Her grunt was laced with intrigue. "Well, fucking congratulations. He's a catch."

The thought of how much of a catch he was made Elaine emotional. She smiled tightly and nodded.

"Oh shit," Fiona said, watching her carefully.

Elaine cleared her throat. "What?"

"You're falling in love with him. You have a

whole new energy about you." Fiona smiled. "It's good, Laney. I'm happy for you. I mean after those four frogs you were going to marry, who never turned into princes, you finally nabbed the one you deserve. And I mean that. You deserve someone great."

Elaine stared at her incredulously. "Really? You really think that?"

Fiona flung her body in Elaine's direction. "Yes. I do. I would follow you to the moon and fucking back and know I would be in good hands." She sat back in her seat. "Listen, I wanted you to make this fucking utopia work. An agency where the sheep lie with the fucking lions. Hungry lions love tender-ass sheep meat. There's no lying with us. We'll eat you alive. But you're a lion too. You're like a vegan lion. There's only one or two of you in existence. So as president of AMTA, I'll devour the meat for you." She folded her arms across her chest. "But listen, I want something for doing this. When you sell, I want a stake in this fucking company, enough to keep my job."

Elaine studied Fiona carefully. With her prissy blond bob and Chanel suits, no one would ever guess she was a barracuda. And she was right. Chewing on raw meat made Elaine sick to her stomach. She hated it. She'd rather fight in court and negotiate a great outcome for the artist who was getting fucked over.

"And you're okay with being co-president with a representative from Mega Link?"

"First, tell me, what percentage of the company are you going to give me as insurance?"

Elaine smirked. She had nothing but respect for Fiona's shrewdness. "Two."

"Five," Fiona countered.

"Three. That's all I can give you. I need to keep my bargaining power."

Fiona nodded as she pondered Elaine's offer.

"Then I'll take it."

The two ladies smiled at each other then got out of their chairs and hugged like two good friends.

FIVE MONTHS LATER

ELAINE AND ZACH WERE RUSHING TO GET DRESSED. Over the last five months, Sonja had kept pushing back her wedding date until finally it was happening, at three o'clock that Saturday. It was now two o'clock.

They'd spent all morning and most of the after-noon in bed, eating, talking, and making love. Whomever Sonja had hired to make Elaine's Pacific Palisades mansion ready for the wedding had free reign of the house and grounds. So Elaine basically moved in with Zach in the Malibu Colonies and had slept in his bed every night since their ordeal with Linus. Elaine knew nothing about the particu-lars of Sonja and Jay's ceremony, and it hadn't been difficult to keep her nose out of it, either.

Sonja had told her the guests were supposed to dress like gypsies. Since Zach was in Sydney and then London from Monday through Thursday, she'd bought both their costumes, and now it was time to see him in the multicolored blousy pants and matching button-down with a V-neck vest.

"Zach, are you ready?" she called from the bathroom, examining herself in the mirror. Her costume included a sheer, off-the-shoulder scarlet-red blouse with bell sleeves and a long, flowing skirt.

"I've been ready, babe," he called from the bedroom.

"Okay, here I come."

She rushed out of the bathroom, and he was sitting on the side of the bed, finishing a casual business call with a guy named Jerry.

"Gotta go. We'll talk Monday," he said, then he ended the call and stood. "You make everything you wear so damn sexy."

Elaine walked over and wrapped her arms around his neck. "Speak for yourself."

Their lips and tongues softly mingled. Every part of Elaine wanted to merge with Zach.

"We should go," he said breathlessly.

"Good idea."

But first he clutched her by the waist, guided her on top of the bed, laid her on her back, lifted her skirt, and slid his rigid erection into her wetness.

⁂

SONJA THREW HER ARMS UP AND SHOOK THEM WHEN she saw Elaine and Zach. "You're late. I was about to ask Jay to go get you."

They had just walked through the front door of Elaine's house.

"Sorry about that," Elaine said and kissed her sister on the cheek. Sonja was dressed in a light-blue outfit that was similar to Elaine's.

"I'm not busting your balls. It's not like you to be so late. I thought you fell off the edge of the world or something." She hugged Zach too.

"As you can see, we're fine," Elaine said. "But why aren't you wearing white? I know you're already married, but aren't you still pretending to be a new bride?"

"Ha, ha, ha," Sonja said then hooked her arm around Elaine's, guiding her along. "Come on, tardy birds. The guests are waiting."

Her own house felt like a foreign palace as they walked under the vaulted ceilings of the hallway. Elaine wondered how she could have ever lived in such an impersonal environment for so long. Come Monday morning, she would have Dena, her real estate agent, place the house on the market. It was obvious that as long as she and Zach were together —and she didn't see an end to their relationship in sight—she wouldn't need to live in her Palisades mansion.

Elaine smiled at Zach, whose skin had turned patchy red. Perhaps he was nervous about being called out for being late. She smiled at him to let him know it was okay. He smirked back, and their gazes remained glued on each other for a few beats.

"Listen, Laney, everything's casual today. We'll go through the rigmarole of things that go on at these sorts of gatherings," she said, rolling her hand nonchalantly. "The guy does this, the girl does that.

The audience applauds. The couple kisses, then we party and dance our lives away," Sonja said without breaking her brisk pace.

Elaine watched her sister as if she had lost her ever-loving mind. "We're talking about a wedding, right?"

"Yes, there's a wedding involved."

Elaine raised her eyebrows at Zach, as if she were asking whether he thought Sonja had gone momentarily insane too. He shrugged, communicating that he didn't know.

"But today is about family and friends So..." They walked out of the house and were facing the back of a massive tent that resembled the dome of a Moorish castle. Soft, beautiful music played from inside, and the notes mingled with the excited sound of voices.

"Zach," Sonja said, watching him with bright, beautiful eyes, "I have never seen my sister happier, and I, we, owe it all to you."

There was something mischievous in Sonja's eyes. It was a look Elaine was all too familiar with. "What's going on, Son?" she asked.

Sonja took her by the hand as she smiled at Zach. "Let me show you."

Elaine was still confused as Sonja guided them

through the back entrance of the tent. When she saw all the people present, her heart nearly stopped, because they were clapping and looking at her.

Her mouth fell open when, through her peripheral vision, she saw Zach drop to his knees.

"What?" she managed to say.

Zach bobbed his hand up and down, signaling everyone to be quiet.

Elaine pressed both hands over her mouth, as she could hardly breathe. It was hard to believe the moment was actually happening.

"So, everybody here knows Jay and I are already married, right?" Sonja asked.

"Yes" came from the entire crowd of what appeared to be a few hundred guests. Elaine focused on the faces of those seated at the large round table up front. She pressed her hand tighter against her mouth when she spotted Zach's mother, Sarah, who was sitting beside a man Elaine recognized as his father. They'd spoken a number of times on the phone, but she had never seen him in the flesh until now.

There was Charlie Lord with Angel. They sat beside the man she recognized as Jack Lord, and the beautiful woman he had his arm around had to be his wife, Daisy. She smiled at Maggie, who smiled back. Maggie was with her husband, Vince Adams, one of the most successful media moguls in the world. Gran was at the table too.

Elaine took a moment to wiggle her fingers at her, and Gran blew her a kiss. Terry was sitting with them, and they blew kisses at each other too. Dexter Frampton, a longtime client, was seated next to Robin. Elaine had to do a double take when she saw another person sitting with their families.

"Riley?" she asked.

It was Jay's sister, the girl who used to be her best friend.

Riley smiled tightly. Elaine knew she was jealous of Elaine's moment, and that was okay. They were connected again by marriage. And now, it was up to Elaine to be the hero and make their friendship good and healthy. She was up for it.

"All right, babe," Zach said, reclaiming her full attention. "Here goes."

He said everything he'd told her a million times already. He knew they were meant to be from the first time he'd laid eyes on her. His soul knew. What he loved most about her was that she'd become his best friend and closest confidante, and next to his parents, she was the smartest person he knew.

"And babe, I'm lucky to be right here, on one

knee, asking you to keep spending the rest of your life with me. That's what I'm asking. Will you marry me?"

Elaine was shaking all over as tears streamed down her face. Her fifth proposal, and he was the only man to get on one knee to make it. Perhaps that was a sign the fifth time was a charm. "Yes," she said at the top of her lungs. "Absolutely!"

Zach picked her up off her feet, and they kissed until her head started spinning. Then he motioned to quiet the guests yet again.

"Elaine?" He slowly lowered her until her feet were back on the ground.

"Yes?" She sounded as intrigued and confused as she knew her face probably expressed.

"Today."

She tilted her head slightly.

"Will you marry me today? Right now. I've already applied for our licenses. We're good, babe."

Elaine gasped. It was so silent, the guests could have heard a pin drop. She blinked hard, a few times, thinking that at any moment, she would wake up. The truth was, she wanted nothing more than to be Zach's wife. Before their passionate kiss in front of friends and family, she'd had a slight fear that Zach too could leave her at the altar, like the others. But now, he was guaranteeing that wouldn't happen.

It took her a moment to realize that her head was nodding, and so her voice caught up. "Yes. Yes, let's do it now."

A woman wearing a minister's collar stood and took a position on a stage in the middle of the space. "Zachary Benjamin Lord, Elaine Marie Hester, please join me."

Each step felt as though Elaine were walking on air. People were clapping and whistling. Her eyes sought out one pair who needed to tell her everything was okay. When she saw her gran, Sonja had her arm around her, and they both were smiling and letting the happy tears roll.

They took their places. Zach held both her hands tightly as he stared into her eyes. Then he smirked. She smiled.

"Two soul mates were never strangers," the minister began. "From birth, you were two souls waiting for the day when you would meet and merge. All of life's circumstances led to this moment, right here. None of your living has been in vain."

The tears were running so much that Elaine could hardly see. And Zach, being the perfect gentleman that he was, halted the minister to make sure someone got Elaine enough tissue so she could wipe her eyes and blow her nose. Her gran did the honors.

Then the minister asked if he took Elaine Marie Hester to be his lawfully married wife.

"Yes, I take the woman of my dreams to be my wife," he said.

"And Elaine, do you take Zachary Benjamin Lord to be your lawfully married husband?"

"Yes, I take this man who I never saw coming and who was my God-given partner to be my husband."

For the first time ever, she saw Zachary Lord cry, and it was beautiful. She used her fingers to wipe the tears from his face. He tugged her against him and told her he loved her.

They were kissing even before the minister pronounced them man and wife, and the minister didn't say he could now kiss his bride—for obvious reasons.

JACQUES BLANCHARD WAS THE NIGHT'S entertainment. There was more dancing than sitting. Everyone's dinner was being served restaurant-style to keep the night from feeling so formal, Sonja had said.

Elaine met both of Zach's parents, and she promised that the two of them would fly to Connecticut and spend time with the Lords soon. Zach had enjoyed dinner with Elaine, Gran, Terry, and Robbie a number of times in the past few months. She learned her sister had had a lot to do with making the night happen, along with Angel, Charlie's wife, who appeared to have become fast and close friends with Sonja.

Many of Elaine's clients were present, and she had to greet them all. She was back to being a lawyer, practicing at her old firm but not as a partner this time, although they wanted her to reclaim her previous senior title. But she'd said no. All she wanted to do was be a lawyer. She no longer needed to be a top dog to feel validated. She caught up with Fiona, who had made an extremely competent company president. They didn't talk business, discussing only how smart Elaine was to have said yes, right on the spot.

"The Laney I used to know would've called all the activities to a halt until she could gain some kind of control over it all." Fiona smiled then cupped the side of Elaine's face. "You've done, like, a ninety-degree change."

Elaine laughed. "Not a one-eighty?"

She shook her head emphatically. "Oh no. Going from one extreme to the other is just extremism. *Reasonable* lives at ninety degrees, and that's where you are."

Elaine smiled.

Goodness, Fiona was right. She had changed. The things that used to make her blow fire and brimstone didn't bother her anymore. Being around Zach was teaching her that she couldn't fight everyone's battles or control every situation. She found herself listening more, which actually prevented her from flying off the handle. Recently, Elaine had heard her reputation around town was changing. People were attributing it to the fact that she was finally getting fucked properly. That was definitely true, but it was more than that.

Zach had so quickly become a reflection of the better parts of herself. When she watched him interact with people in business and in life, he spoke to them respectfully and regarded whatever they had to say as if he was open to learning in a way that could transform his entire belief system if need be. Elaine knew the way he behaved was exactly the way God wanted her to be. And so she wisely chose to imitate him.

"Thanks, Fi, I'm really thankful you've noticed the change in me. Zach has been the perfect partner."

Fiona gazed at Zach with eyes that smoldered. "Plus, fucking him can change Medusa into Aphrodite. My God, look at him."

Elaine tossed her head back and laughed. When she turned her attention on Zach, he was watching her with amusement.

It felt as though it took literally all night to greet their guests. It was after midnight when Elaine and Zach finally ended up in each other's arms for only their second dance of the night. Yet not one guest had left yet. Jacques Blanchard's band took all their instruments off the speakers to keep the noise levels down so couples could canoodle to his softer music and flawless voice.

"Mrs. Lord, you look so beautiful tonight," Zach said in her ear and then kissed her forehead.

"Thank you, my love," she said.

"Mmm," he said. "I love the sound of that. Call me that more often."

"I will, my love."

He kissed her tenderly.

"So…" he said with his eyes closed and then breathed in deeply. "So how does three point two billion sound?"

"It depends on what you mean," she said, although she thought she had an idea.

"We have a buyer who's ready to purchase your shares of AMTA for three point two billion."

Elaine's mouth was open for a moment. "No way. Already? The last valuation had me at one point nine billion, and that was only three weeks ago."

He grinned proudly. "We had four sharks on the hook. Volt Media Corp came in the highest. They're pretty legit."

"And they agreed to keep Fiona on as president?"

"They'll offer her a five-year contract, which she could break at any time."

"Ten years."

"I'm sure they'll be okay with that. Fiona's kicked ass in the last five months. Plus she has her three percent interest. That was smart of you to give it to her. However, you have to accept…"

"I accept," she said.

Zach beamed at her. "Then the deal is as good as done."

Elaine took a deep breath and released it slowly. It felt as though a two-ton gorilla had jumped off her shoulders. She was free of AMTA, which was why she felt as light as a flower as she glided on the dance floor, led by Zach, her forever lover.

MOST OF THE GUESTS HAD FINALLY GONE HOME around four in the morning, and mostly family remained. Charlie brought out his guitar, and they sat around the fire pit as he played, and they all talked and made plans to get together again in the future. The most interesting banter was between Robbie and Dexter. She would make a comment, and he would make a contrary statement. He would say something, and Robbie would negate it.

"Could you two just get a room already?" Maggie asked.

And on that note, Robbie faked a yawn and said, "Speaking of a room. I have a flight in"—she checked her watch—"soon."

Dexter looked so disappointed as she hugged and kissed everyone but him and left. Robbie was definitely sending him a message, and Elaine was surprised to see her behave that way. It wasn't like her at all, which meant she must've actually liked Dexter.

At six o'clock in the morning, they all went their separate ways. Zach hadn't taken Elaine home, though. They caught a flight to a mysterious destination to begin their weeklong honeymoon.

It was no sweat off Elaine's back to reschedule her clients until she returned. She wanted to go on as many adventures with Zach as one lifetime would allow. And as he slowly separated her from her clothes after the airplane darted down the runway and climbed to their flying altitude, she knew one thing for certain. Zach would always bring overwhelming pleasure to her body, and it was about to start—now.

ALSO BY Z.L. ARKADIE

CONTEMPORARY ROMANCE SERIES

LOVE IN THE USA (THE HESTERS)

ONCE FRIENDS (**A HOLLYWOOD LOVE STORY**) SONJA & JAY #1

NOW LOVERS (**A HOLLYWOOD LOVE STORY**) SONJA & JAY #2

TAMING THE SHREWD (**ANOTHER HOLLYWOOD LOVE STORY**) ELAINE & ZACH

WAITING ON YOU (A BROOKLYN LOVE STORY) **ROBIN & DEXTER**

WINNER TAKES LOVE (A SEATTLE LOVE STORY) THERESA & GREG

LOVE IN THE USA (THE LORDS)

FIND HER, KEEP HER - A MARTHA'S VINEYARD LOVE STORY, **BOOK 1**

There's Something About Her, A Manhattan Love Story, **Book 2**

Say You Love Her, An LA Love Story, **Book 3**

Know Her, Love Her (Daisy & Belmont, #1), **Book 4**

Still In Love With Her (Maggie & Vince, #1), **Book 5**

Explore Her, More of Her (Daisy & Belmont, #2), **Book 6**

Made To Like Her (Maggie & Vince, #2), **Book 7**

He's So Bad: A San Francisco Love Story, **Book 8**

Made To Love Her (Maggie & Vince, #3) **Book 9**

He's So Good (Robert & Carter) **Book 10**

Say You Love Me (Charlie & Angel) **Book 11**

Adore Her, More of Her (Daisy & Belmont, #3) **Book 12**

HER PERFECT MAN

Authors Z.L. Arkadie & T.R. Bertrand

The Boss' Desire

The Artist's Love

The Professor's Heart

The Chef's Passion

ROMANTIC SUSPENSE SERIES

THE STERLINGS

Secrets & Chance, **Book 1**

Revelations, **Book 2**

Forever and Ever, **Book 3**

The Secret Keeper, **Book 4**

PARANORMAL ROMANCE SERIES

PARCHED

Parched **Book 1**

The Seventh Sister

Quenched **Book 2**

The Fifth Sister

Ignite (Includes "Light Speed") **Book 3**

Vanquish, **Book 4**

Steal With A Kiss, **Book 5**

Forget Me Never (Pt. I) **Book 6**

Forget Me Never (Pt. 2) **Book 7**

ABOUT THE AUTHOR

I'm a city girl/desert rat born and raised in Southern California, who grew up loving to daydream. I've traveled a lot and lived in different cities around the country, which taught me how different we all are. The biggest lesson I've learned is that we are all more than cliches and stereotypes, and I write to capture our truths in my stories.

I also love to cook. I love a fine dining experience, you know *Top Chef* style, but without the fine dining price tag. And I love a good book that has the power to take me someplace I've never been. But most of all, I love authentic displays of kindness within myself and others.

For more information:
zlarkadiebooks.com
contact@zlarkadiebooks.com